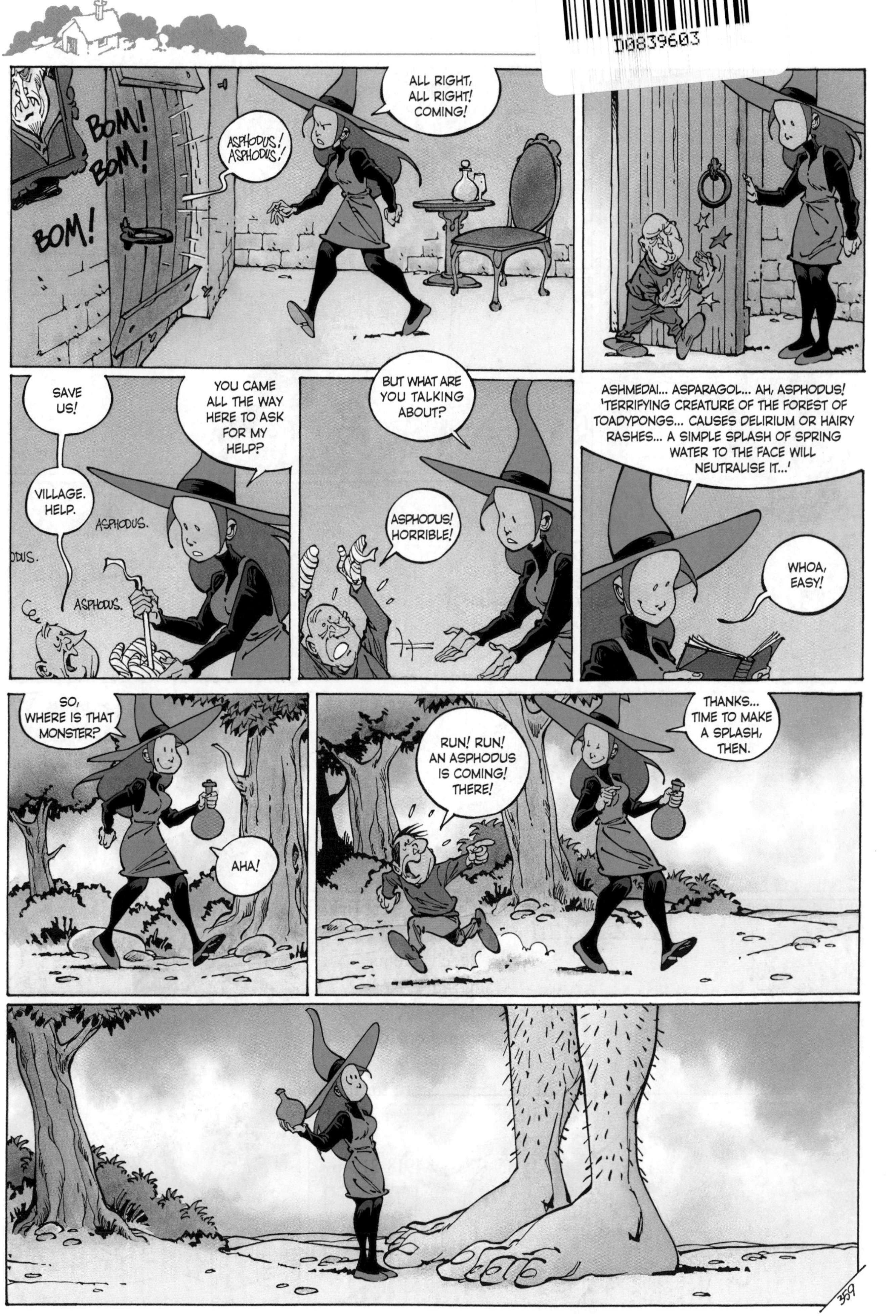
BOM! BOM!
BOM!
ASPHODUS! ASPHODUS!
ALL RIGHT, ALL RIGHT! COMING!
SAVE US!
VILLAGE. HELP.
ASPHODUS.
DUS.
ASPHODUS.
YOU CAME ALL THE WAY HERE TO ASK FOR MY HELP?
BUT WHAT ARE YOU TALKING ABOUT?
ASPHODUS! HORRIBLE!
ASHMEDAI... ASPARAGOL... AH, ASPHODUS! 'TERRIFYING CREATURE OF THE FOREST OF TOADYPONGS... CAUSES DELIRIUM OR HAIRY RASHES... A SIMPLE SPLASH OF SPRING WATER TO THE FACE WILL NEUTRALISE IT...'
WHOA, EASY!
SO, WHERE IS THAT MONSTER?
AHA!
RUN! RUN! AN ASPHODUS IS COMING! THERE!
THANKS... TIME TO MAKE A SPLASH, THEN.

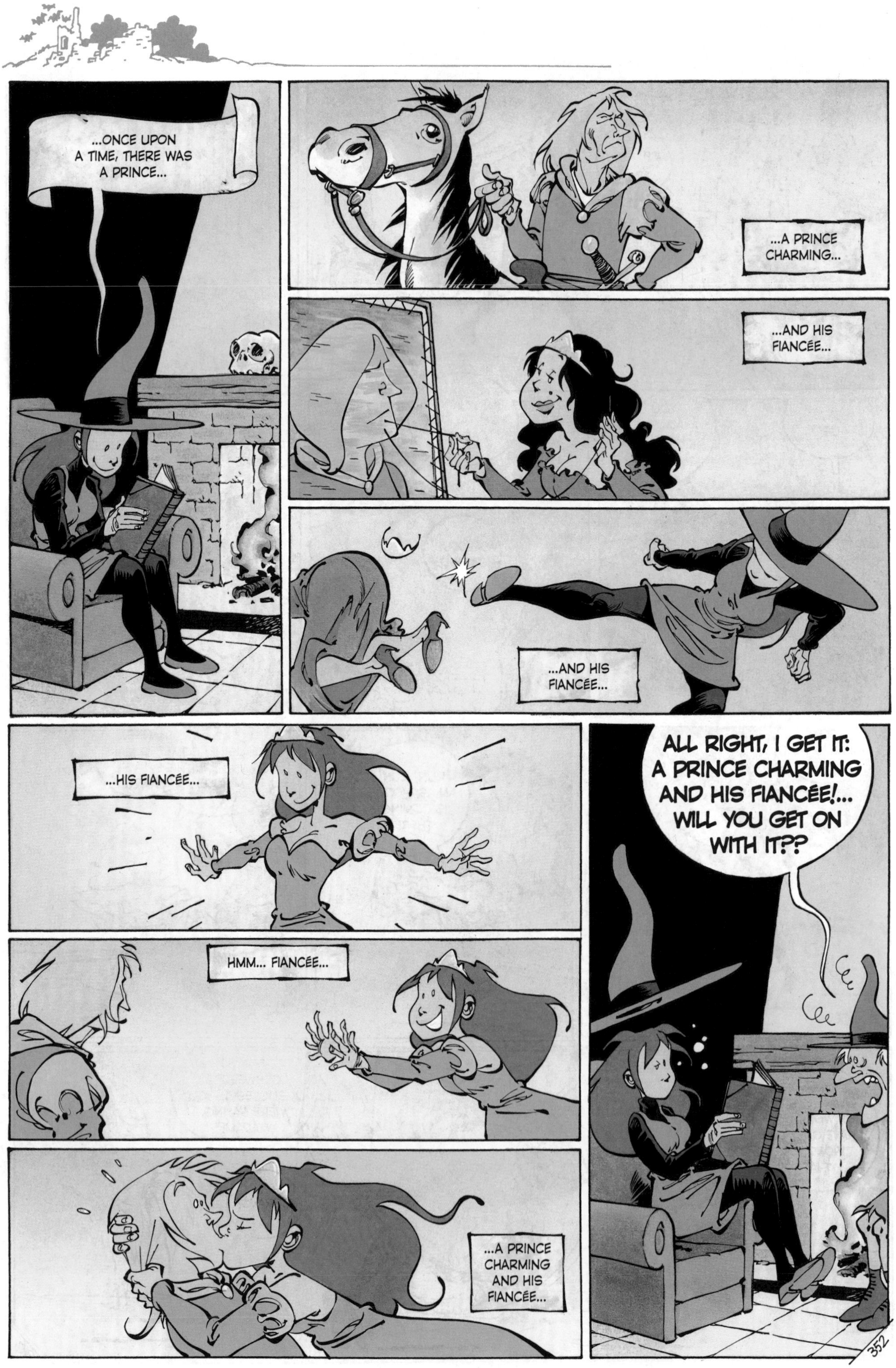
...ONCE UPON A TIME, THERE WAS A PRINCE...
...A PRINCE CHARMING...
...AND HIS FIANCÉE...
...AND HIS FIANCÉE...
...HIS FIANCÉE...
HMM... FIANCÉE...
...A PRINCE CHARMING AND HIS FIANCÉE...
ALL RIGHT, I GET IT: A PRINCE CHARMING AND HIS FIANCÉE!... WILL YOU GET ON WITH IT??
352

Melusine

Tales of the Full Moon

Colours : Cerise

5

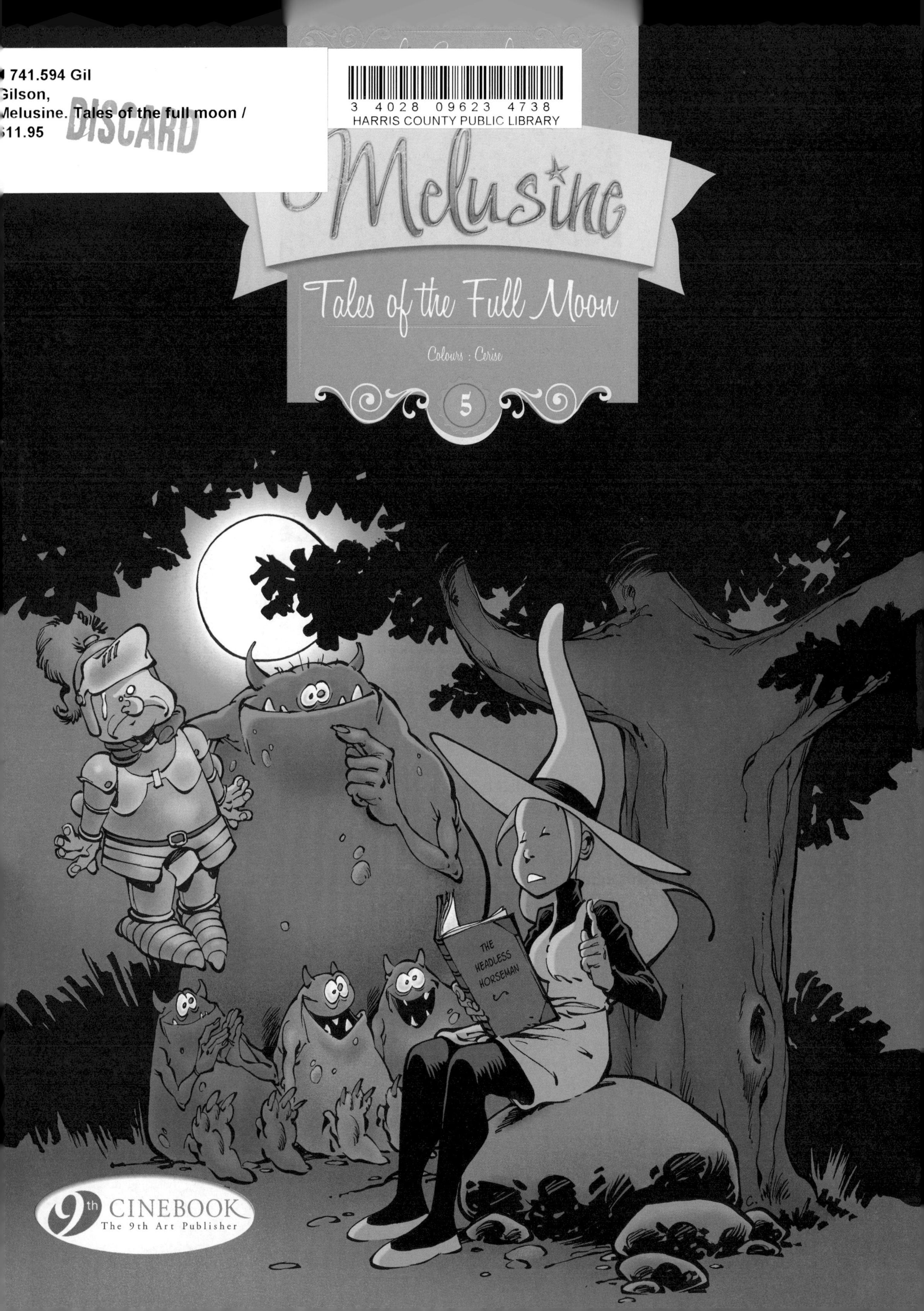
THE HEADLESS HORSEMAN
9th CINEBOOK
The 9th Art Publisher

Original title: Mélusine 10 – Contes de la pleine Lune
Original edition: © Dupuis 2002
by Clarke & Gilson
www.dupuis.com

English translation: © 2014 Cinebook Ltd

Translator: Jerome Saincantin
Lettering and text layout: Design Amorandi
Printed in Spain by Just Colour Graphic

This edition first published in Great Britain in 2014 by
Cinebook Ltd
56 Beech Avenue
Canterbury, Kent
CT4 7TA
www.cinebook.com

A CIP catalogue record for this book
is available from the British Library

ISBN 978-1-84918-212-6

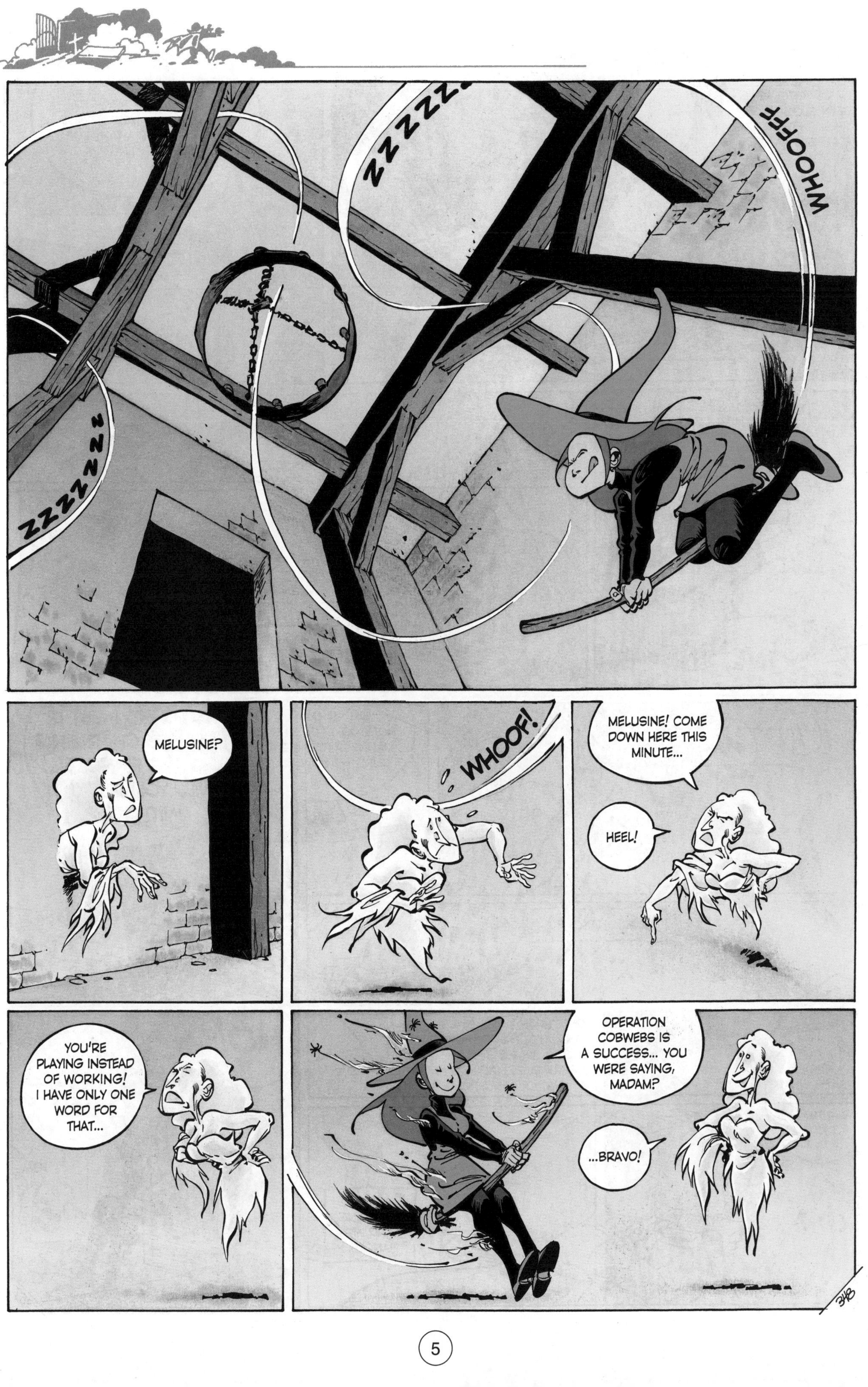
ZZZZZ
WHOOFFF
ZZZZZZZ
MELUSINE?
WHOOF!
MELUSINE! COME DOWN HERE THIS MINUTE...
HEEL!
YOU'RE PLAYING INSTEAD OF WORKING! I HAVE ONLY ONE WORD FOR THAT...
OPERATION COBWEBS IS A SUCCESS... YOU WERE SAYING, MADAM?
...BRAVO!

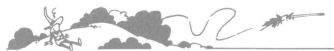

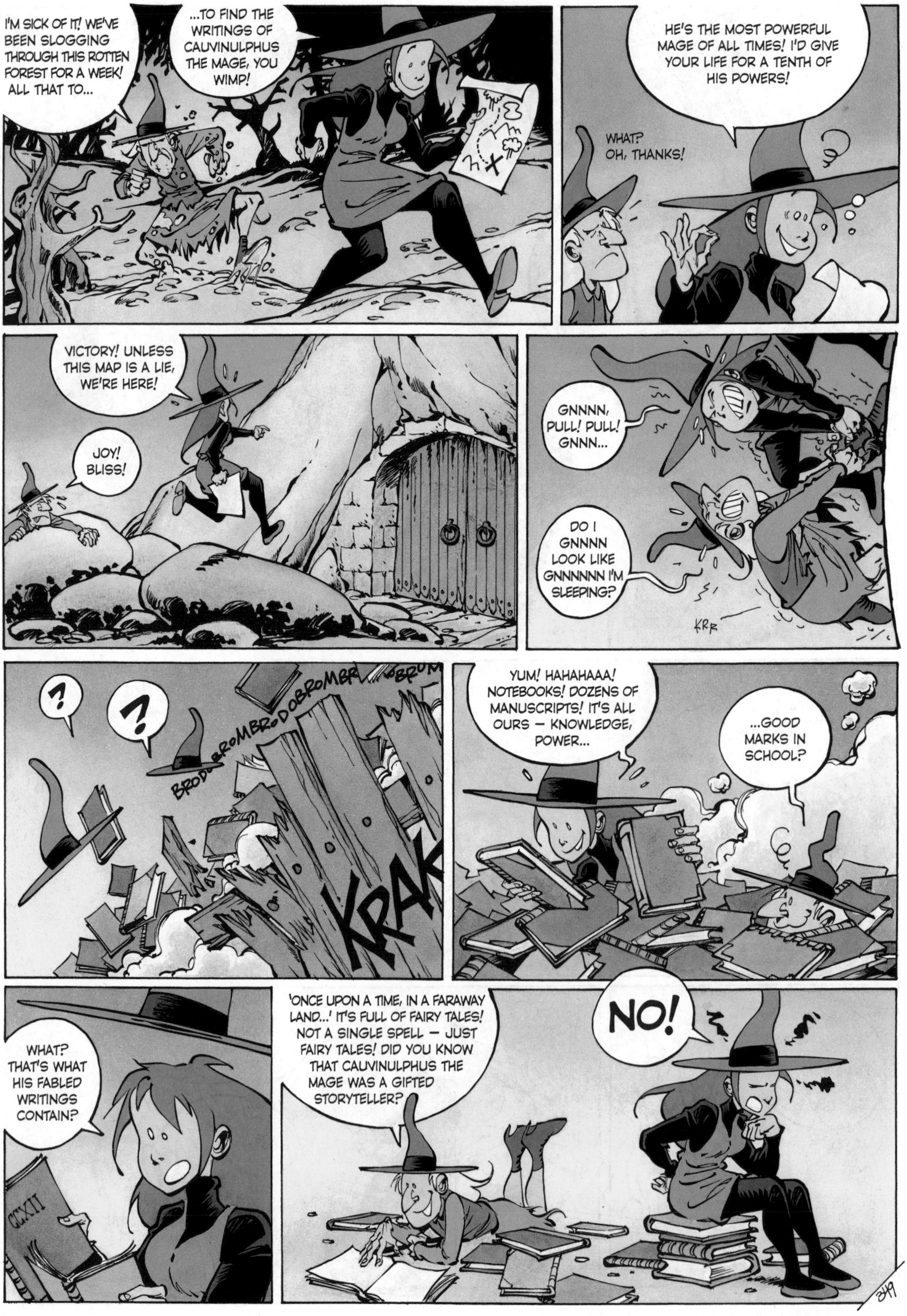
I'M SICK OF IT! WE'VE BEEN SLOGGING THROUGH THIS ROTTEN FOREST FOR A WEEK! ALL THAT TO...
...TO FIND THE WRITINGS OF CAUVINULPHUS THE MAGE, YOU WIMP!
HE'S THE MOST POWERFUL MAGE OF ALL TIMES! I'D GIVE YOUR LIFE FOR A TENTH OF HIS POWERS!
WHAT? OH, THANKS!
VICTORY! UNLESS THIS MAP IS A LIE, WE'RE HERE!
JOY! BLISS!
GNNNN, PULL! PULL! GNNN...
DO I GNNNN LOOK LIKE GNNNNNN I'M SLEEPING?
KRR
?
?
KRAK
YUM! HAHAHAAA! NOTEBOOKS! DOZENS OF MANUSCRIPTS! IT'S ALL OURS — KNOWLEDGE, POWER...
...GOOD MARKS IN SCHOOL?
WHAT? THAT'S WHAT HIS FABLED WRITINGS CONTAIN?
CCXII
'ONCE UPON A TIME, IN A FARAWAY LAND...' IT'S FULL OF FAIRY TALES! NOT A SINGLE SPELL — JUST FAIRY TALES! DID YOU KNOW THAT CAUVINULPHUS THE MAGE WAS A GIFTED STORYTELLER?
NO!

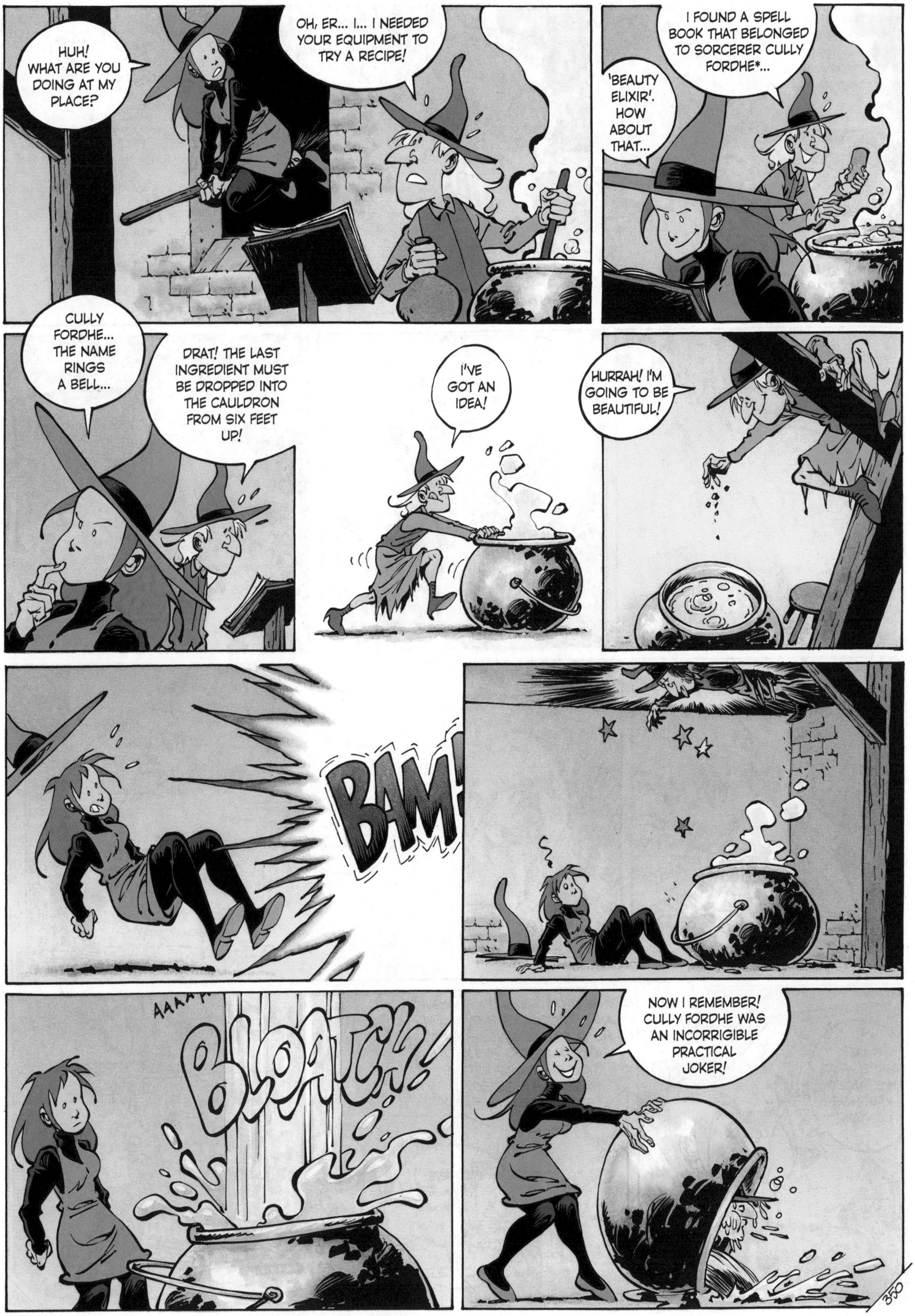
HUH! WHAT ARE YOU DOING AT MY PLACE?
OH, ER... I... I NEEDED YOUR EQUIPMENT TO TRY A RECIPE!
I FOUND A SPELL BOOK THAT BELONGED TO SORCERER CULLY FORDHE*...
'BEAUTY ELIXIR'. HOW ABOUT THAT...
CULLY FORDHE... THE NAME RINGS A BELL...
DRAT! THE LAST INGREDIENT MUST BE DROPPED INTO THE CAULDRON FROM SIX FEET UP!
I'VE GOT AN IDEA!
HURRAH! I'M GOING TO BE BEAUTIFUL!
BAM
AAAA
BLOATCH!
NOW I REMEMBER! CULLY FORDHE WAS AN INCORRIGIBLE PRACTICAL JOKER!
350

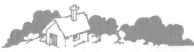

*CULLIFORD, PIERRE — ALSO KNOWN AS PEYO: CREATOR OF THE SMURFS.

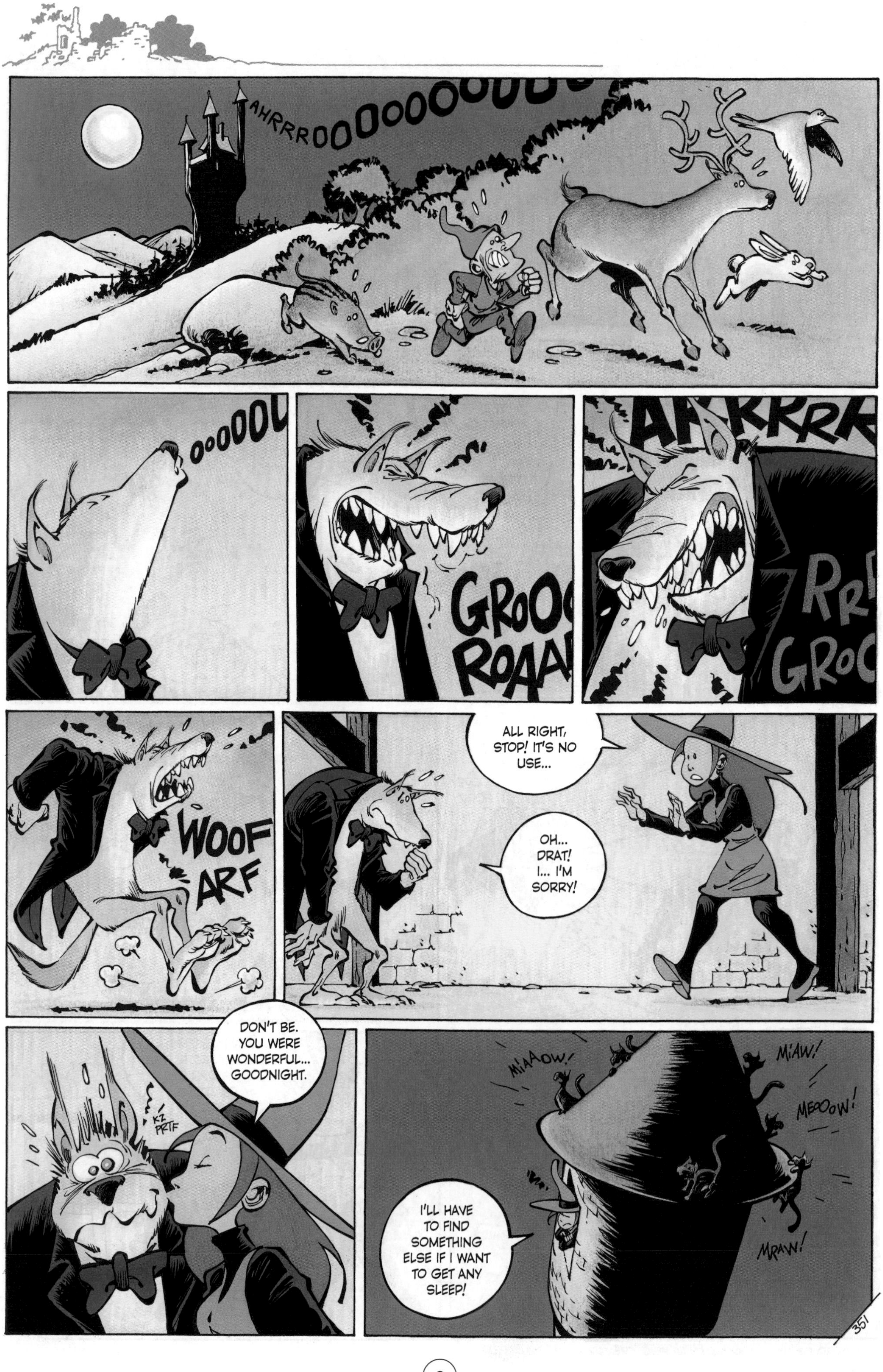
AHRRROOOOOOOOUUUU
OOOOOOU
GROOO
ROAAA
AHRRRR
RRR
GROO
WOOF
ARF
ALL RIGHT, STOP! IT'S NO USE...
OH... DRAT! I... I'M SORRY!
DON'T BE. YOU WERE WONDERFUL... GOODNIGHT.
KZ PRTF
MIAAOW!
MIAW!
MEOOOW!
I'LL HAVE TO FIND SOMETHING ELSE IF I WANT TO GET ANY SLEEP!
MRAW!
351

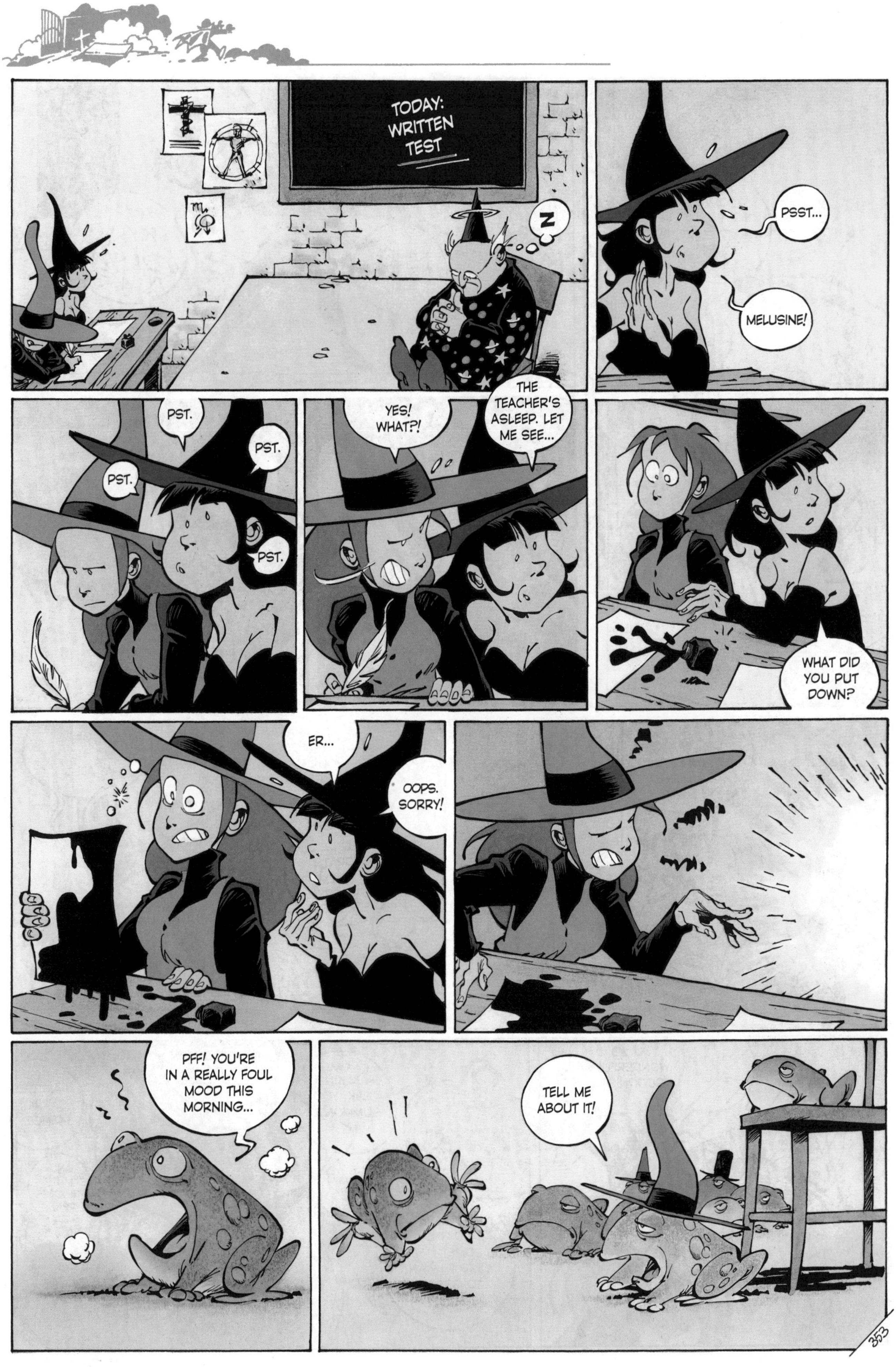
TODAY:
WRITTEN
TEST
Z
PSST...
MELUSINE!
PST.
PST.
PST.
PST.
YES! WHAT?!
THE TEACHER'S ASLEEP. LET ME SEE...
WHAT DID YOU PUT DOWN?
ER...
OOPS. SORRY!
PFF! YOU'RE IN A REALLY FOUL MOOD THIS MORNING...
TELL ME ABOUT IT!
353

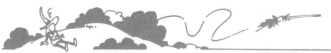

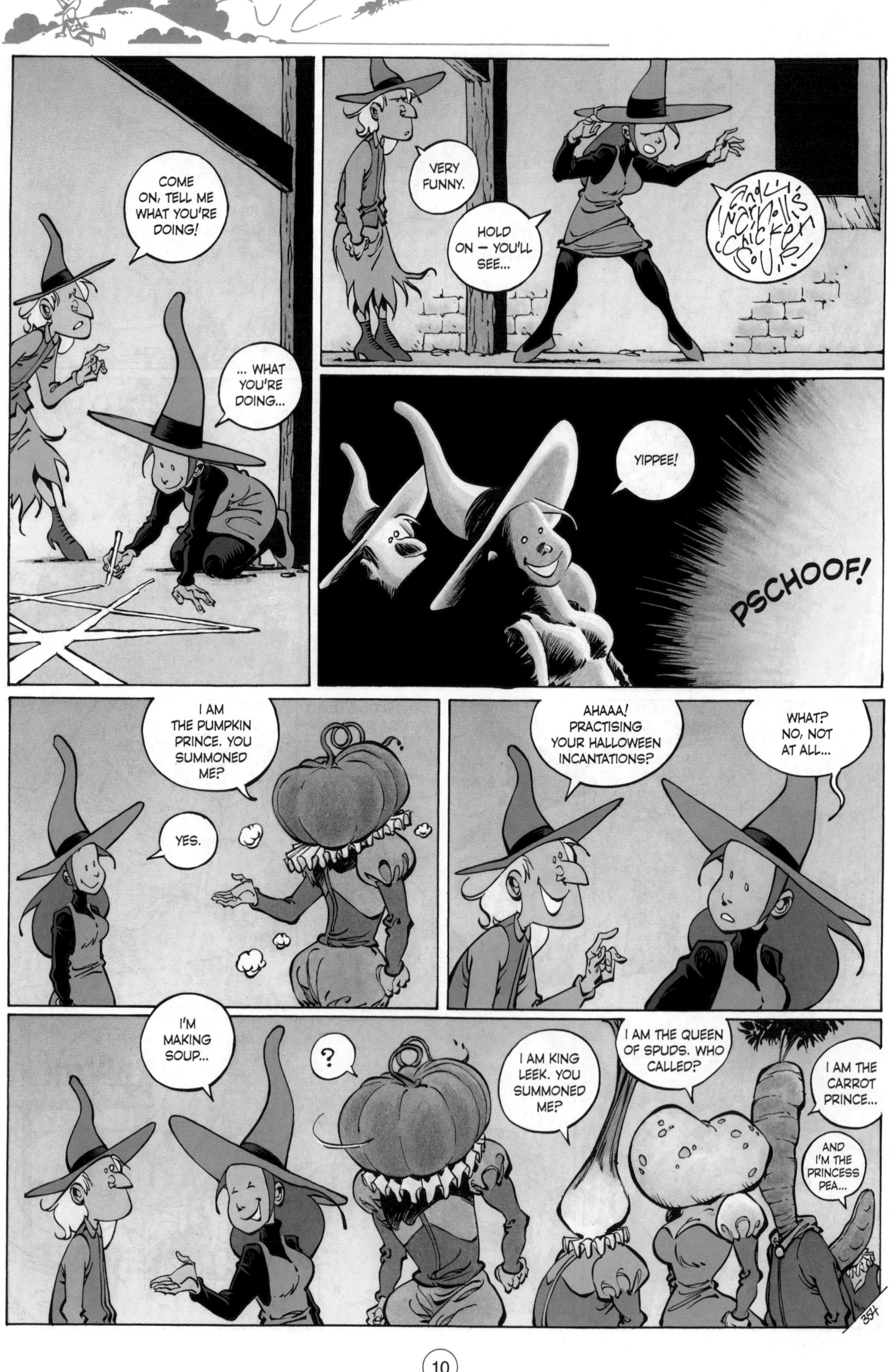
COME ON, TELL ME WHAT YOU'RE DOING!
... WHAT YOU'RE DOING...
VERY FUNNY.
HOLD ON — YOU'LL SEE...
YIPPEE!
PSCHOOF!
I AM THE PUMPKIN PRINCE. YOU SUMMONED ME?
YES.
AHAAA! PRACTISING YOUR HALLOWEEN INCANTATIONS?
WHAT? NO, NOT AT ALL...
I'M MAKING SOUP...
?
I AM KING LEEK. YOU SUMMONED ME?
I AM THE QUEEN OF SPUDS. WHO CALLED?
I AM THE CARROT PRINCE...
AND I'M THE PRINCESS PEA...

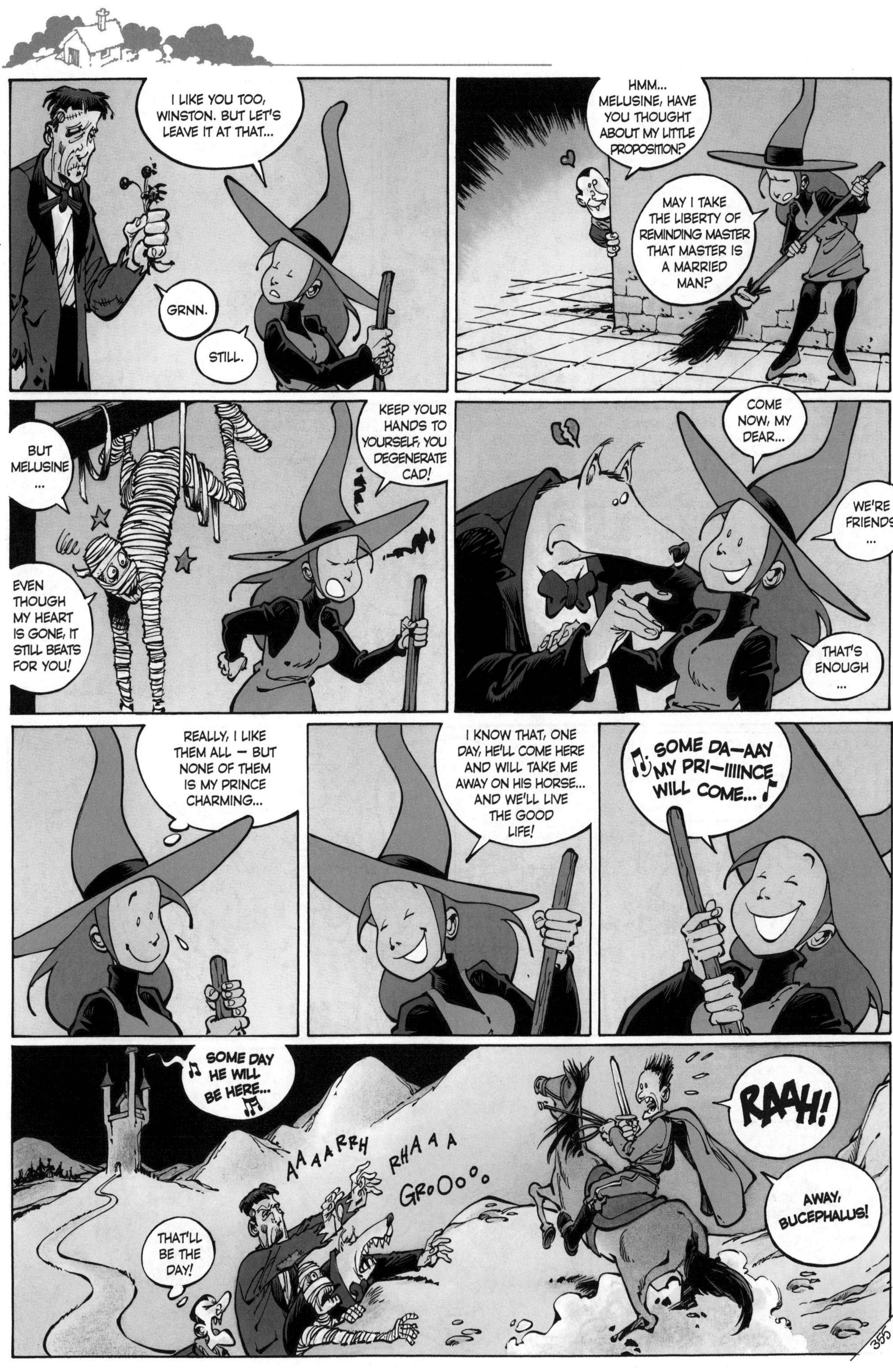
I LIKE YOU TOO, WINSTON. BUT LET'S LEAVE IT AT THAT...
GRNN.
STILL.
HMM... MELUSINE, HAVE YOU THOUGHT ABOUT MY LITTLE PROPOSITION?
MAY I TAKE THE LIBERTY OF REMINDING MASTER THAT MASTER IS A MARRIED MAN?
BUT MELUSINE ...
EVEN THOUGH MY HEART IS GONE, IT STILL BEATS FOR YOU!
KEEP YOUR HANDS TO YOURSELF, YOU DEGENERATE CAD!
COME NOW, MY DEAR...
WE'RE FRIENDS ...
THAT'S ENOUGH ...
REALLY, I LIKE THEM ALL — BUT NONE OF THEM IS MY PRINCE CHARMING...
I KNOW THAT, ONE DAY, HE'LL COME HERE AND WILL TAKE ME AWAY ON HIS HORSE... AND WE'LL LIVE THE GOOD LIFE!
SOME DA—AAY MY PRI—IIIINCE WILL COME...
SOME DAY HE WILL BE HERE...
AAAARRH
RHAAA
GROOOo
THAT'LL BE THE DAY!
RAAH!
AWAY, BUCEPHALUS!
355

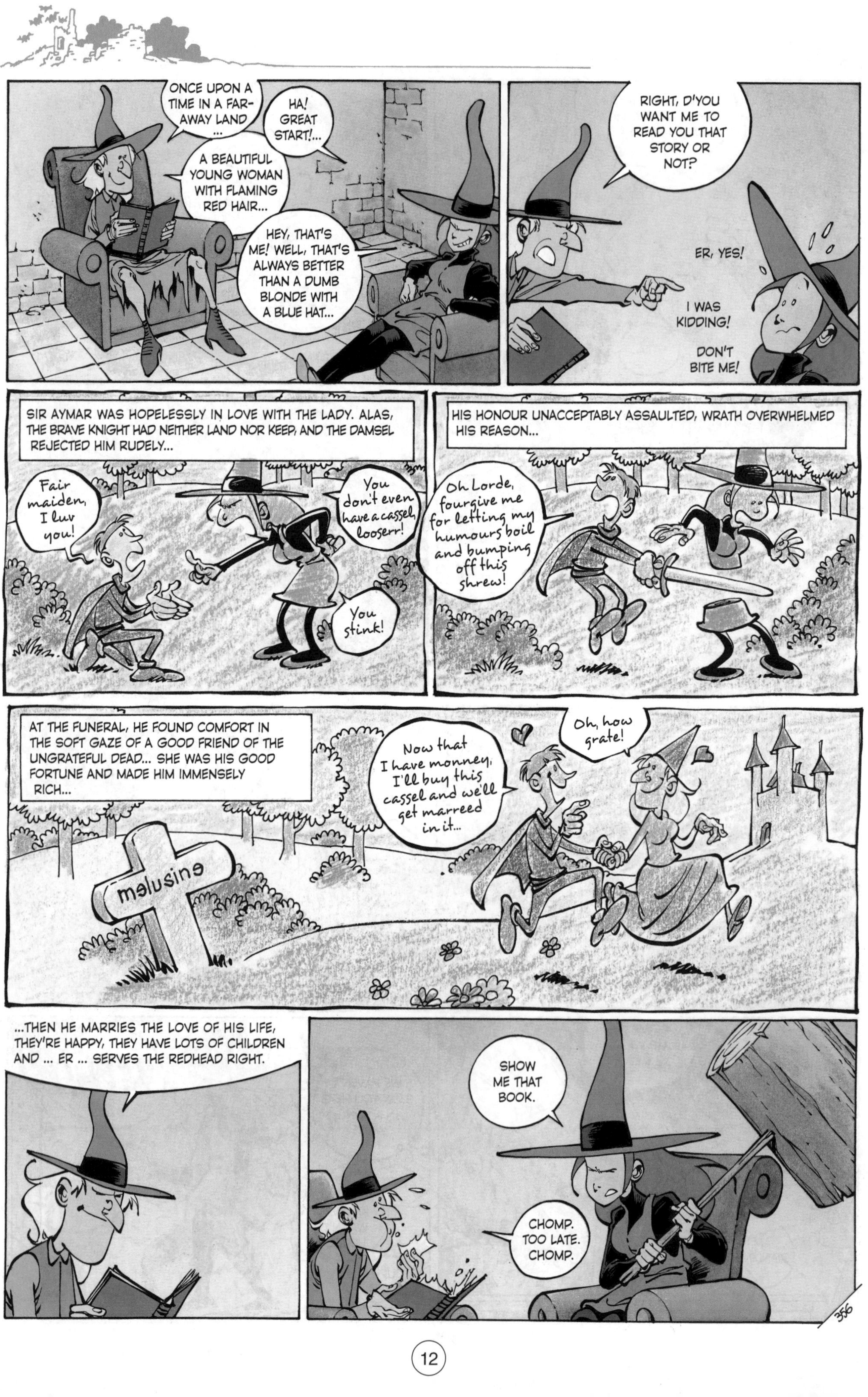

ONCE UPON A TIME IN A FAR-AWAY LAND ...
HA! GREAT START!...
A BEAUTIFUL YOUNG WOMAN WITH FLAMING RED HAIR...
HEY, THAT'S ME! WELL, THAT'S ALWAYS BETTER THAN A DUMB BLONDE WITH A BLUE HAT...
RIGHT, D'YOU WANT ME TO READ YOU THAT STORY OR NOT?
ER, YES!
I WAS KIDDING!
DON'T BITE ME!
SIR AYMAR WAS HOPELESSLY IN LOVE WITH THE LADY. ALAS, THE BRAVE KNIGHT HAD NEITHER LAND NOR KEEP, AND THE DAMSEL REJECTED HIM RUDELY...
Fair maiden, I luv you!
You don't even have a cassel, looserr!
You stink!
HIS HONOUR UNACCEPTABLY ASSAULTED, WRATH OVERWHELMED HIS REASON...
Oh Lorde, fourgive me for letting my humours boil and bumping off this shrew!
AT THE FUNERAL, HE FOUND COMFORT IN THE SOFT GAZE OF A GOOD FRIEND OF THE UNGRATEFUL DEAD... SHE WAS HIS GOOD FORTUNE AND MADE HIM IMMENSELY RICH...
melusine
Now that I have monney, I'll buy this cassel and we'll get marreed in it...
Oh, how grate!
...THEN HE MARRIES THE LOVE OF HIS LIFE, THEY'RE HAPPY, THEY HAVE LOTS OF CHILDREN AND ... ER ... SERVES THE REDHEAD RIGHT.
SHOW ME THAT BOOK.
CHOMP. TOO LATE. CHOMP.
356

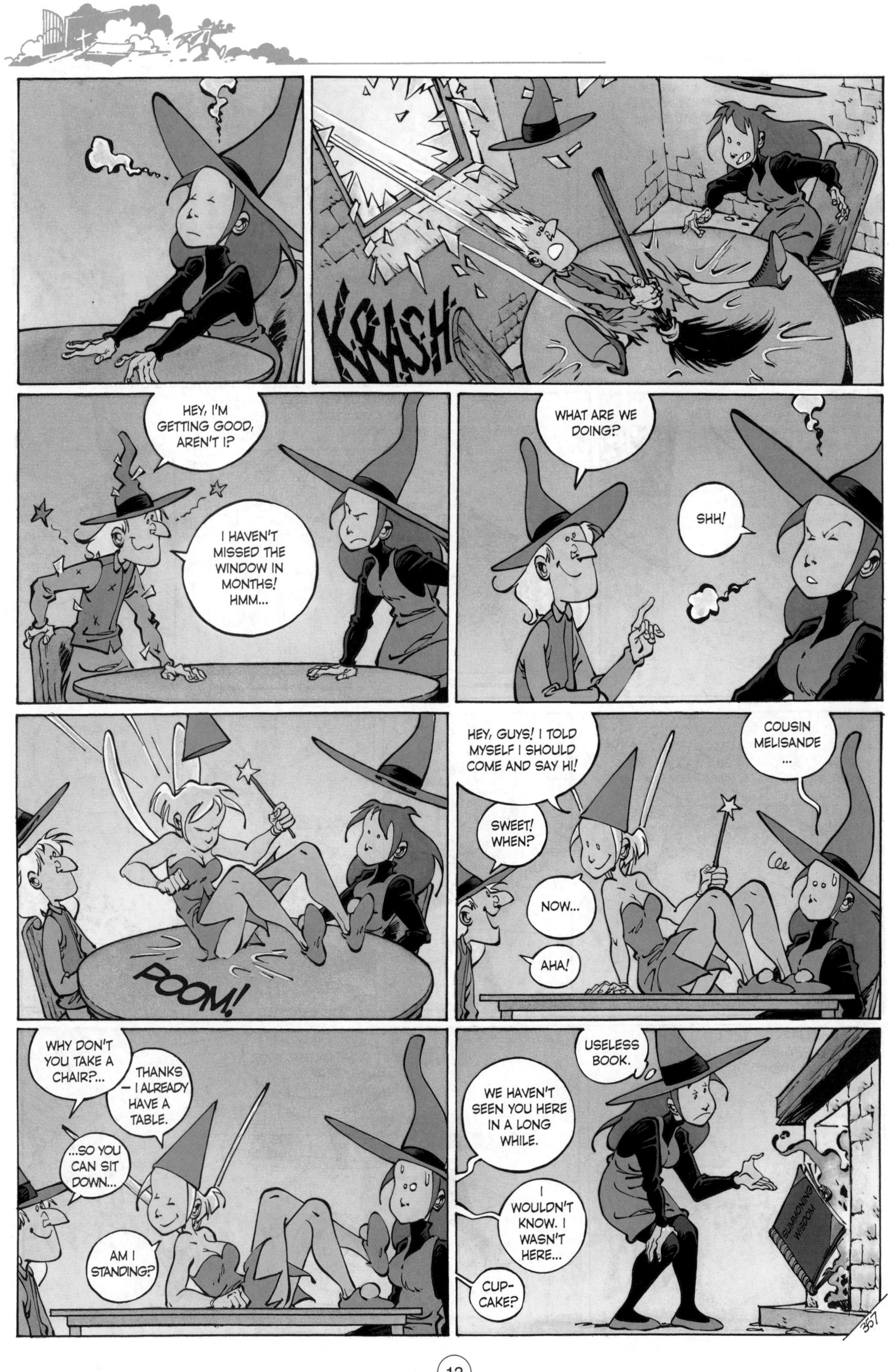
KRASH
HEY, I'M GETTING GOOD, AREN'T I?
I HAVEN'T MISSED THE WINDOW IN MONTHS! HMM...
WHAT ARE WE DOING?
SHH!
POOM!
HEY, GUYS! I TOLD MYSELF I SHOULD COME AND SAY HI!
COUSIN MELISANDE ...
SWEET! WHEN?
NOW...
AHA!
WHY DON'T YOU TAKE A CHAIR?...
THANKS – I ALREADY HAVE A TABLE.
...SO YOU CAN SIT DOWN...
AM I STANDING?
USELESS BOOK.
WE HAVEN'T SEEN YOU HERE IN A LONG WHILE.
I WOULDN'T KNOW. I WASN'T HERE...
CUP-CAKE?
SUMMONING WISDOM
357

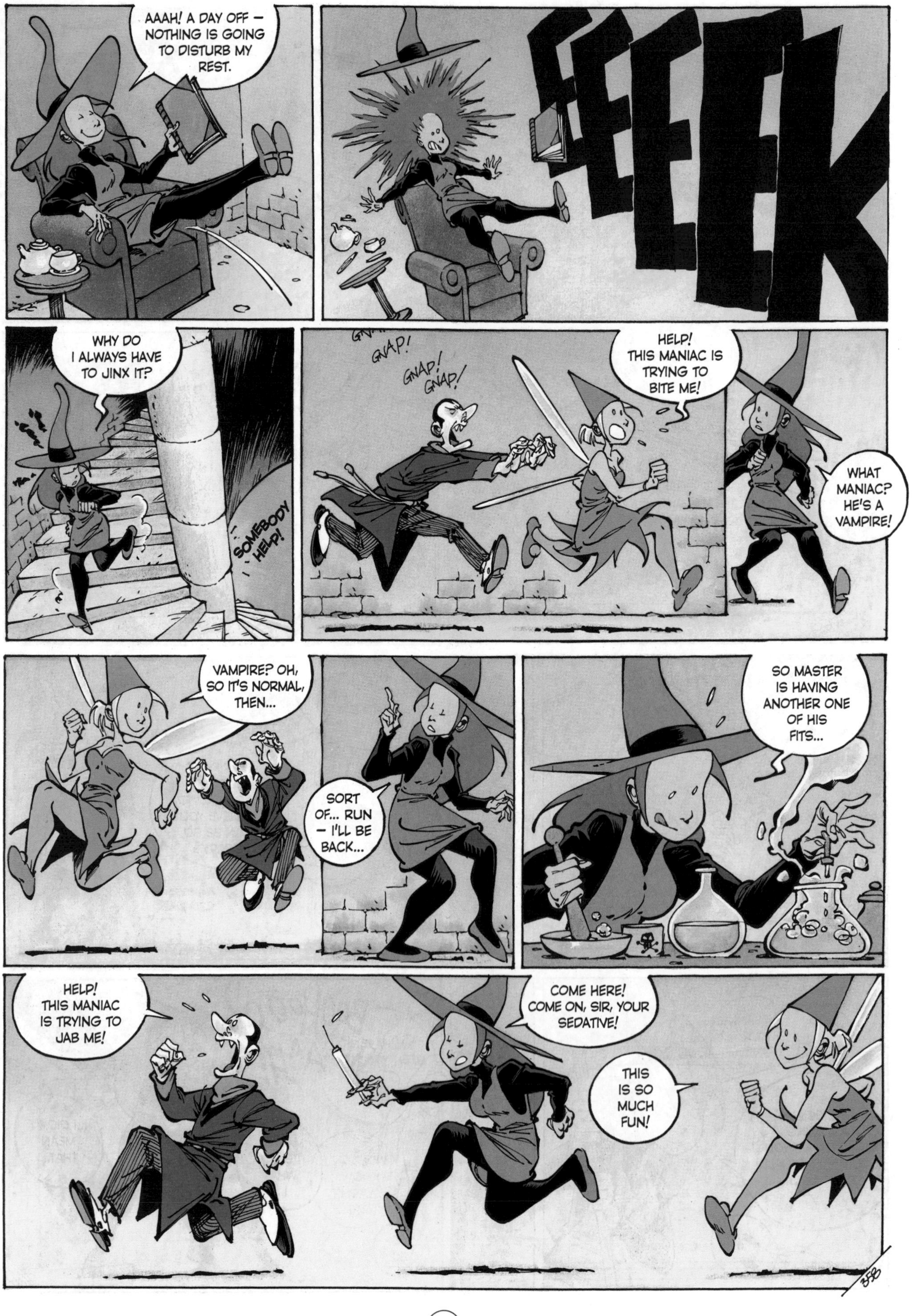

AAAH! A DAY OFF — NOTHING IS GOING TO DISTURB MY REST.
EEEEK
WHY DO I ALWAYS HAVE TO JINX IT?
SOMEBODY HELP!
GNAP! GNAP! GNAP! GNAP!
HELP! THIS MANIAC IS TRYING TO BITE ME!
WHAT MANIAC? HE'S A VAMPIRE!
VAMPIRE? OH, SO IT'S NORMAL, THEN...
SORT OF... RUN — I'LL BE BACK...
SO MASTER IS HAVING ANOTHER ONE OF HIS FITS...
HELP! THIS MANIAC IS TRYING TO JAB ME!
COME HERE! COME ON, SIR, YOUR SEDATIVE!
THIS IS SO MUCH FUN!

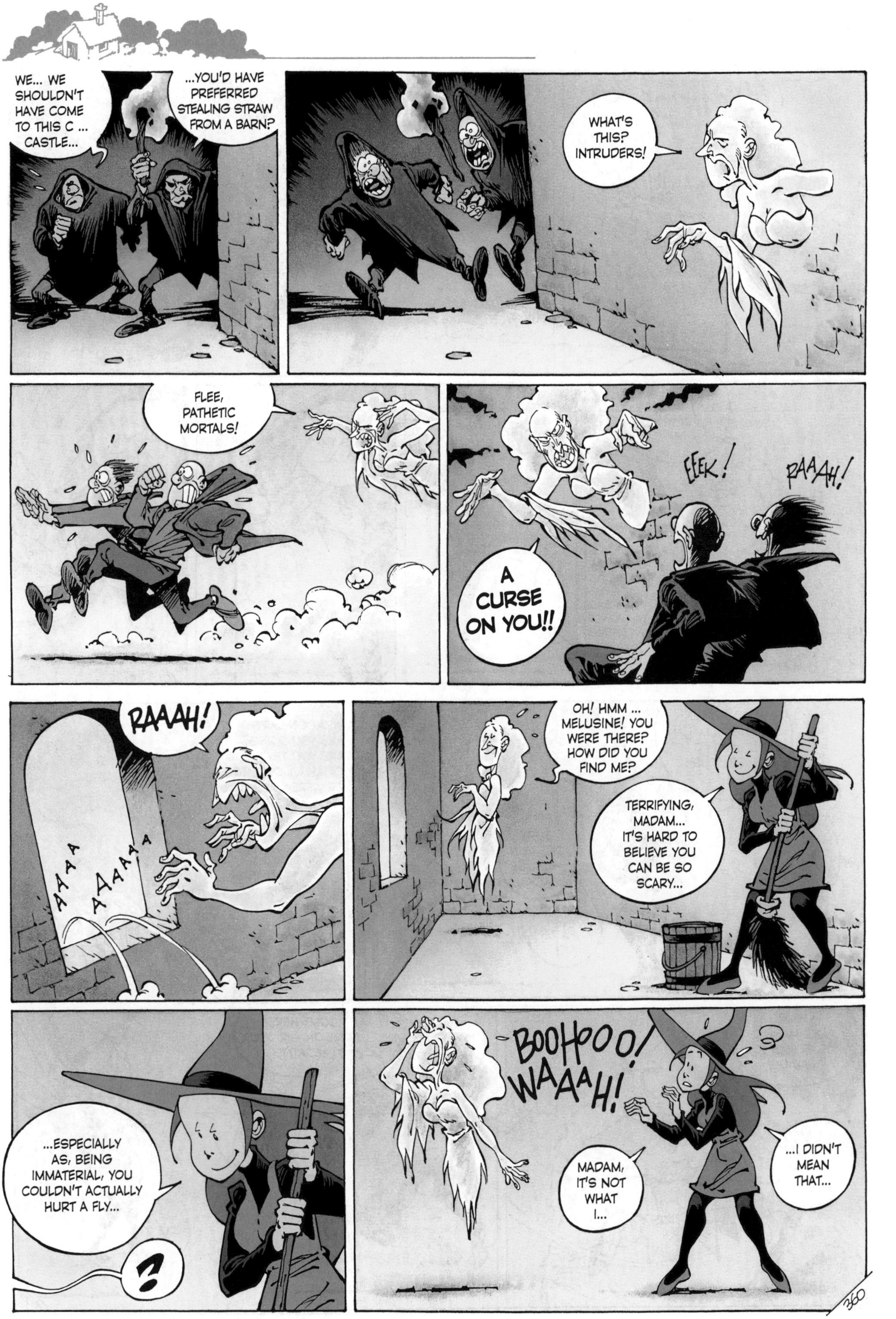

WE... WE SHOULDN'T HAVE COME TO THIS C ... CASTLE...
...YOU'D HAVE PREFERRED STEALING STRAW FROM A BARN?
WHAT'S THIS? INTRUDERS!
FLEE, PATHETIC MORTALS!
A CURSE ON YOU!!
EEEK!
RAAAH!
RAAAH!
AAA AAAAA
OH! HMM ... MELUSINE! YOU WERE THERE? HOW DID YOU FIND ME?
TERRIFYING, MADAM... IT'S HARD TO BELIEVE YOU CAN BE SO SCARY...
...ESPECIALLY AS, BEING IMMATERIAL, YOU COULDN'T ACTUALLY HURT A FLY...
?
BOOHOOO! WAAAH!
MADAM, IT'S NOT WHAT I...
...I DIDN'T MEAN THAT...
360

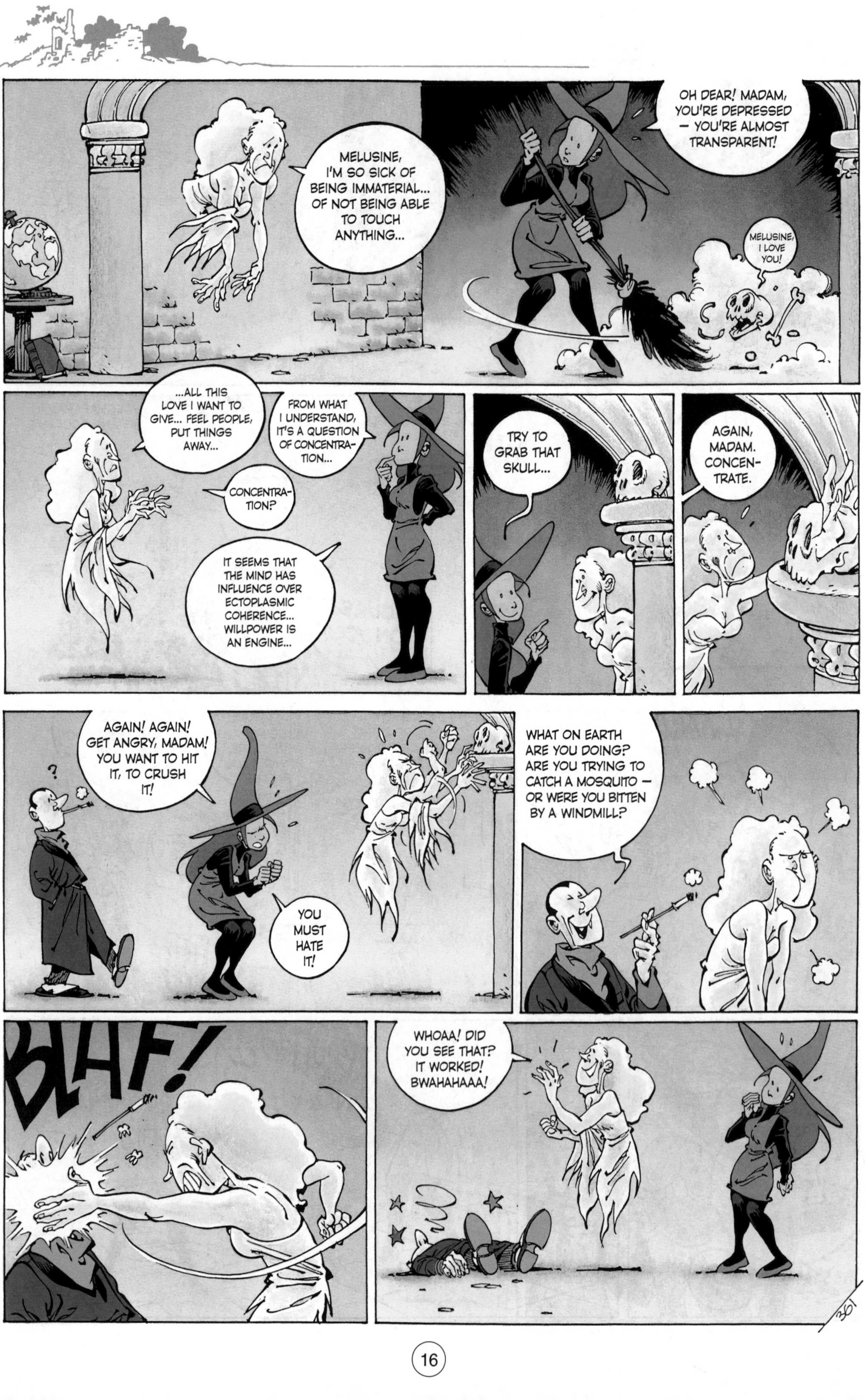
MELUSINE, I'M SO SICK OF BEING IMMATERIAL... OF NOT BEING ABLE TO TOUCH ANYTHING...
OH DEAR! MADAM, YOU'RE DEPRESSED – YOU'RE ALMOST TRANSPARENT!
MELUSINE, I LOVE YOU!
...ALL THIS LOVE I WANT TO GIVE... FEEL PEOPLE, PUT THINGS AWAY...
FROM WHAT I UNDERSTAND, IT'S A QUESTION OF CONCENTRA-TION...
CONCENTRA-TION?
IT SEEMS THAT THE MIND HAS INFLUENCE OVER ECTOPLASMIC COHERENCE... WILLPOWER IS AN ENGINE...
TRY TO GRAB THAT SKULL...
AGAIN, MADAM. CONCEN-TRATE.
?
AGAIN! AGAIN! GET ANGRY, MADAM! YOU WANT TO HIT IT, TO CRUSH IT!
YOU MUST HATE IT!
WHAT ON EARTH ARE YOU DOING? ARE YOU TRYING TO CATCH A MOSQUITO – OR WERE YOU BITTEN BY A WINDMILL?
BLAF!
WHOAA! DID YOU SEE THAT? IT WORKED! BWAHAHAAA!

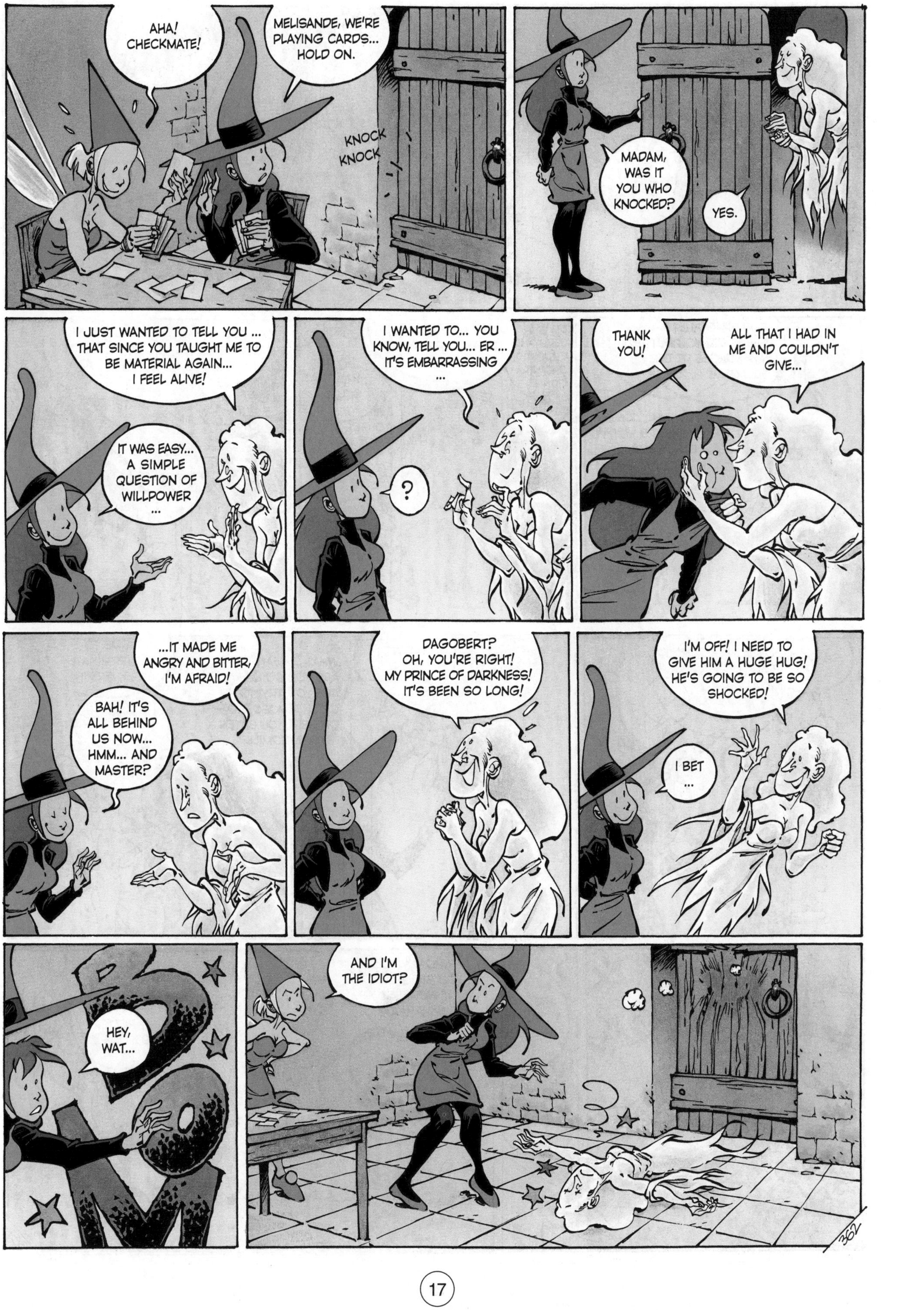
AHA! CHECKMATE!
MELISANDE, WE'RE PLAYING CARDS... HOLD ON.
KNOCK KNOCK
MADAM, WAS IT YOU WHO KNOCKED?
YES.
I JUST WANTED TO TELL YOU ... THAT SINCE YOU TAUGHT ME TO BE MATERIAL AGAIN... I FEEL ALIVE!
IT WAS EASY... A SIMPLE QUESTION OF WILLPOWER ...
I WANTED TO... YOU KNOW, TELL YOU... ER ... IT'S EMBARRASSING ...
?
THANK YOU!
ALL THAT I HAD IN ME AND COULDN'T GIVE...
...IT MADE ME ANGRY AND BITTER, I'M AFRAID!
BAH! IT'S ALL BEHIND US NOW... HMM... AND MASTER?
DAGOBERT? OH, YOU'RE RIGHT! MY PRINCE OF DARKNESS! IT'S BEEN SO LONG!
I'M OFF! I NEED TO GIVE HIM A HUGE HUG! HE'S GOING TO BE SO SHOCKED!
I BET ...
HEY, WAT...
AND I'M THE IDIOT?

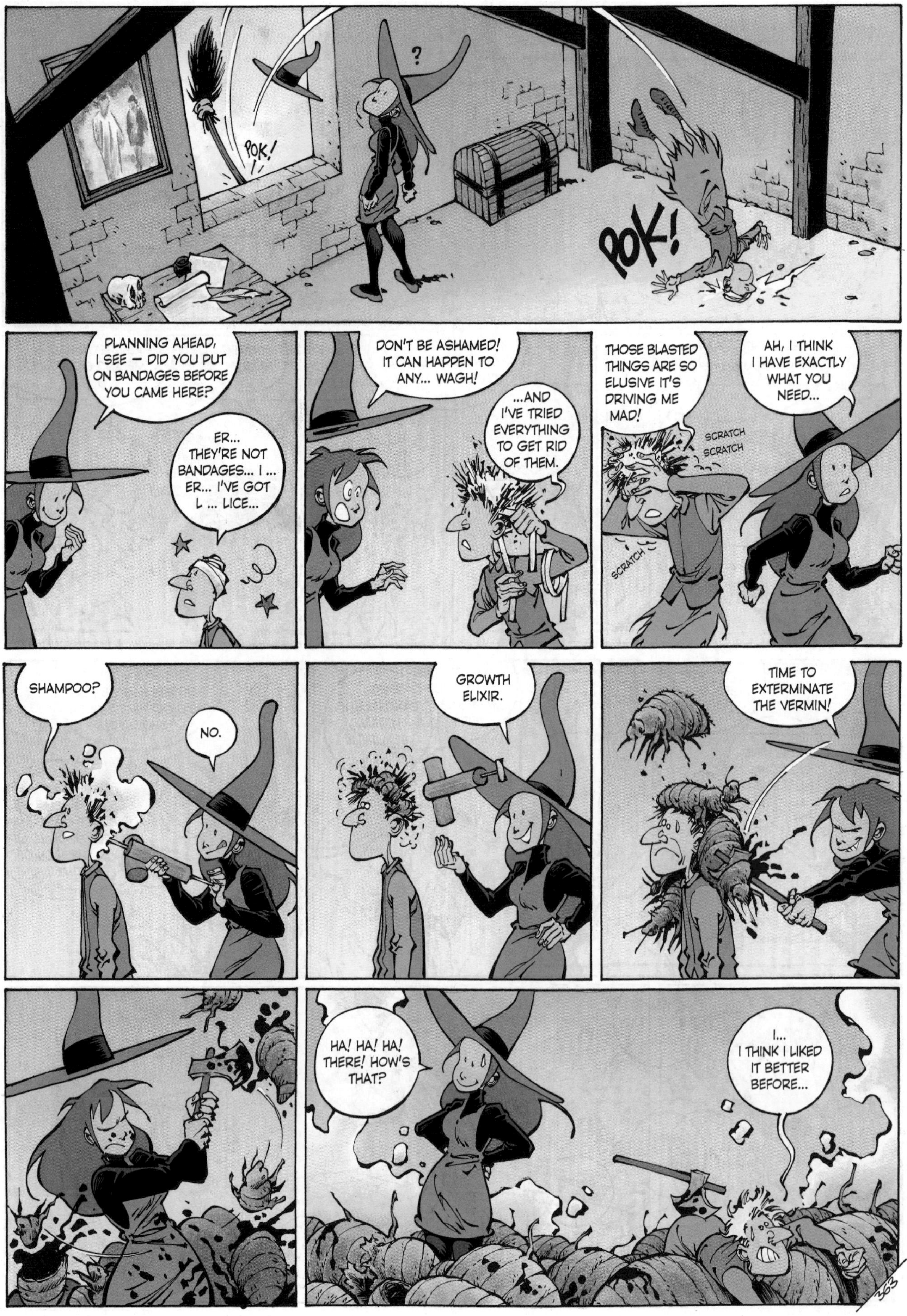
?
POK!
POK!
PLANNING AHEAD, I SEE — DID YOU PUT ON BANDAGES BEFORE YOU CAME HERE?
ER... THEY'RE NOT BANDAGES... I ... ER... I'VE GOT L ... LICE...
DON'T BE ASHAMED! IT CAN HAPPEN TO ANY... WAGH!
...AND I'VE TRIED EVERYTHING TO GET RID OF THEM.
THOSE BLASTED THINGS ARE SO ELUSIVE IT'S DRIVING ME MAD!
SCRATCH SCRATCH
SCRATCH
AH, I THINK I HAVE EXACTLY WHAT YOU NEED...
SHAMPOO?
NO.
GROWTH ELIXIR.
TIME TO EXTERMINATE THE VERMIN!
HA! HA! HA! THERE! HOW'S THAT?
I... I THINK I LIKED IT BETTER BEFORE...

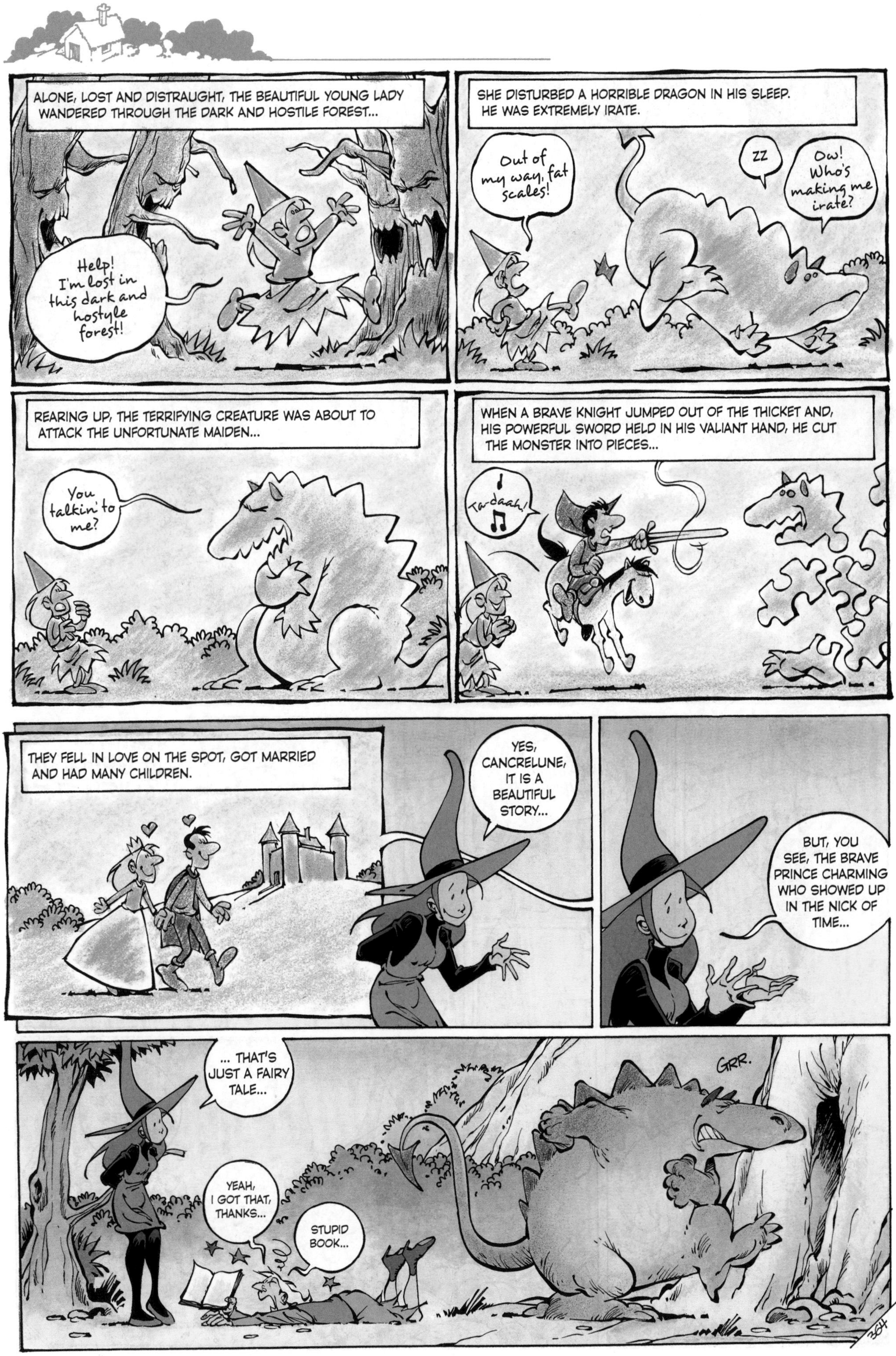

ALONE, LOST AND DISTRAUGHT, THE BEAUTIFUL YOUNG LADY WANDERED THROUGH THE DARK AND HOSTILE FOREST...
Help! I'm lost in this dark and hostyle forest!
SHE DISTURBED A HORRIBLE DRAGON IN HIS SLEEP. HE WAS EXTREMELY IRATE.
Out of my way, fat scales!
ZZ
Ow! Who's making me irate?
REARING UP, THE TERRIFYING CREATURE WAS ABOUT TO ATTACK THE UNFORTUNATE MAIDEN...
You talkin' to me?
WHEN A BRAVE KNIGHT JUMPED OUT OF THE THICKET AND, HIS POWERFUL SWORD HELD IN HIS VALIANT HAND, HE CUT THE MONSTER INTO PIECES...
Ta-daah!
THEY FELL IN LOVE ON THE SPOT, GOT MARRIED AND HAD MANY CHILDREN.
YES, CANCRELUNE, IT IS A BEAUTIFUL STORY...
BUT, YOU SEE, THE BRAVE PRINCE CHARMING WHO SHOWED UP IN THE NICK OF TIME...
... THAT'S JUST A FAIRY TALE...
GRR.
YEAH, I GOT THAT, THANKS...
STUPID BOOK...

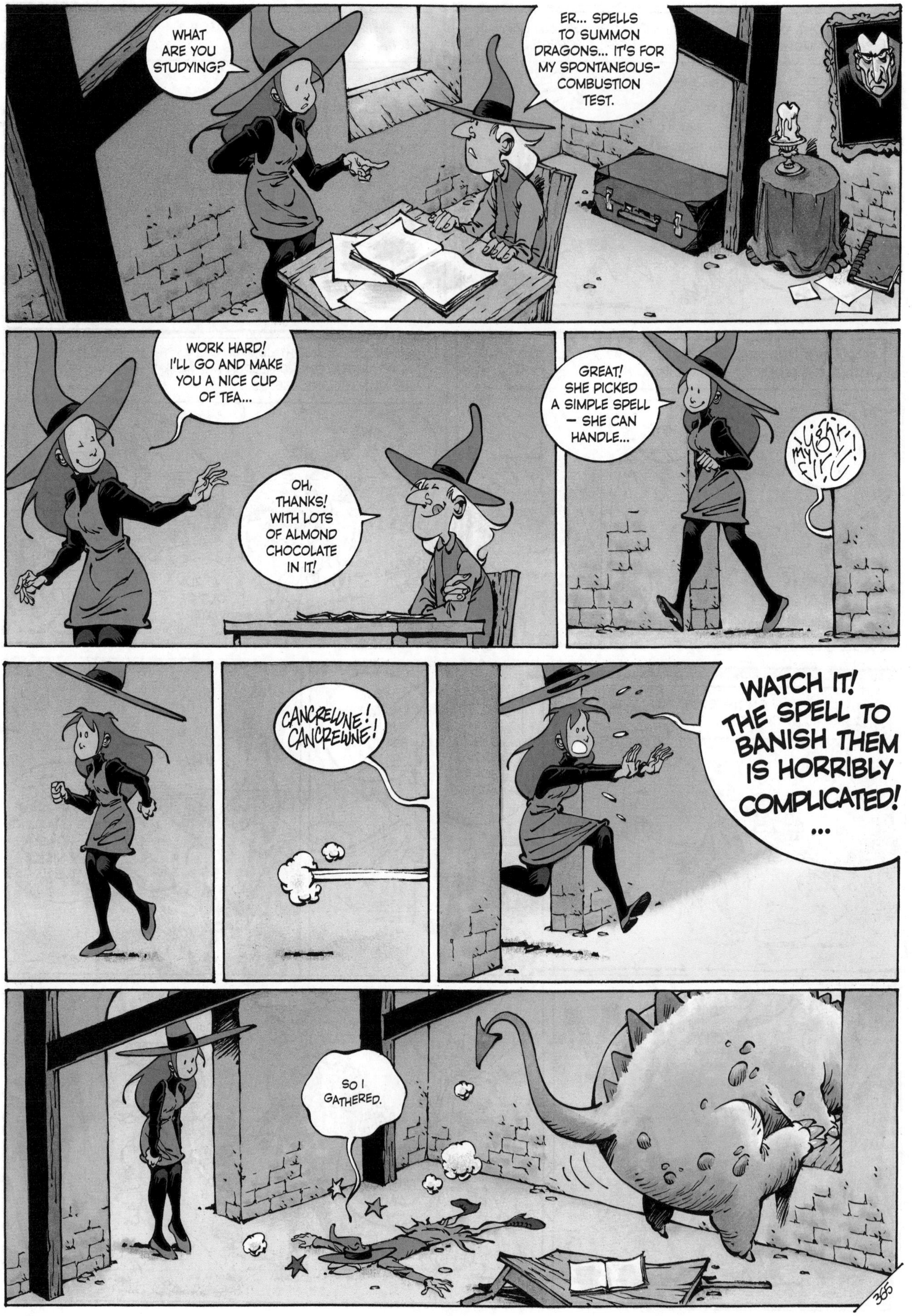
WHAT ARE YOU STUDYING?
ER... SPELLS TO SUMMON DRAGONS... IT'S FOR MY SPONTANEOUS-COMBUSTION TEST.
WORK HARD! I'LL GO AND MAKE YOU A NICE CUP OF TEA...
OH, THANKS! WITH LOTS OF ALMOND CHOCOLATE IN IT!
GREAT! SHE PICKED A SIMPLE SPELL – SHE CAN HANDLE...
CANCREWNE! CANCREWNE!
WATCH IT! THE SPELL TO BANISH THEM IS HORRIBLY COMPLICATED! ...
SO I GATHERED.

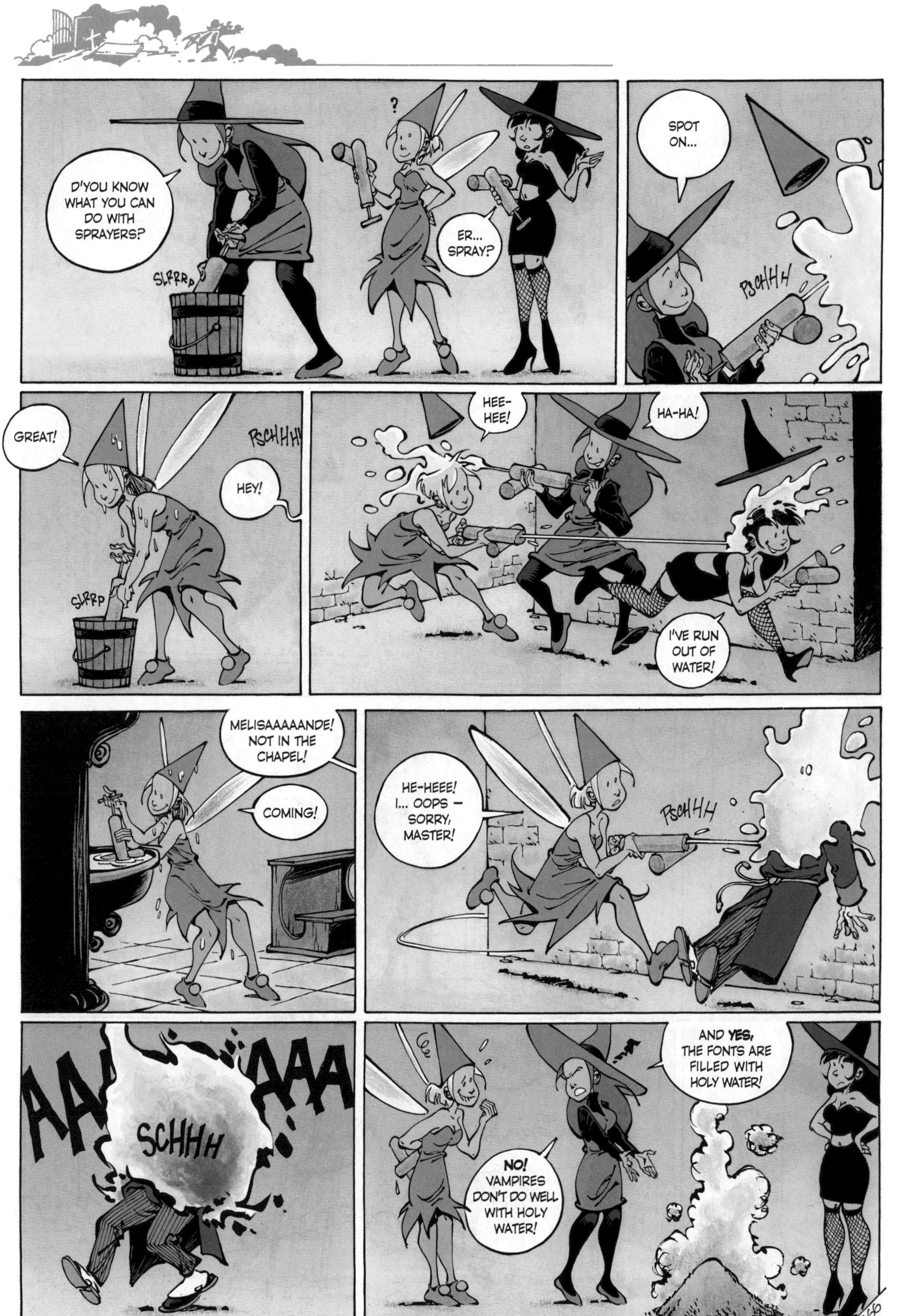
D'YOU KNOW WHAT YOU CAN DO WITH SPRAYERS?
SLRRRP
?
ER... SPRAY?
SPOT ON...
PSCHHH
GREAT!
PSCHHH
HEY!
SLRRP
HEE-HEE!
HA-HA!
I'VE RUN OUT OF WATER!
MELISAAAAANDE! NOT IN THE CHAPEL!
COMING!
HE-HEEE! I... OOPS – SORRY, MASTER!
PSCHHH
AAAAAAA
SCHHH
AND YES, THE FONTS ARE FILLED WITH HOLY WATER!
NO! VAMPIRES DON'T DO WELL WITH HOLY WATER!

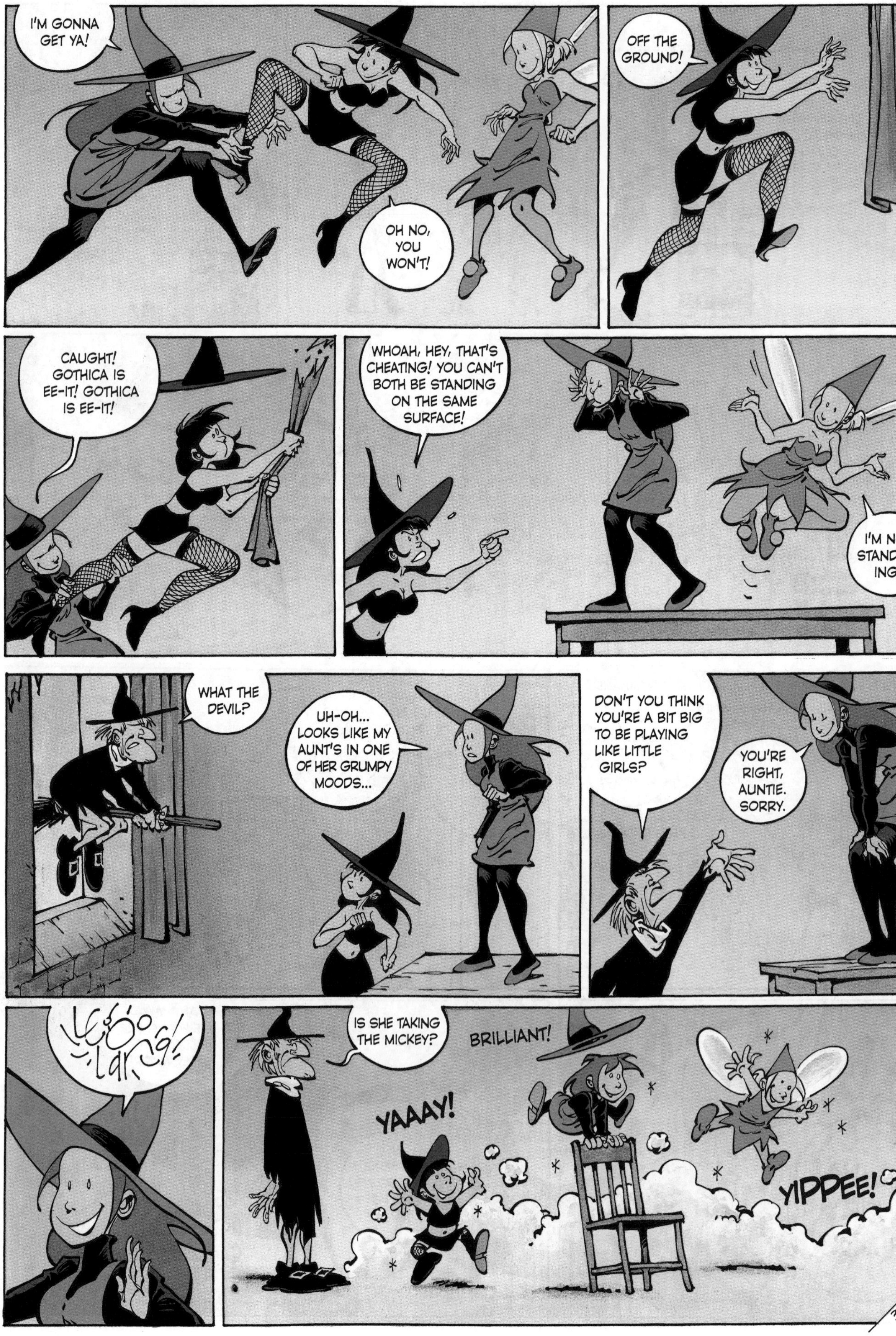
I'M GONNA GET YA!
OH NO, YOU WON'T!
OFF THE GROUND!
CAUGHT! GOTHICA IS EE-IT! GOTHICA IS EE-IT!
WHOAH, HEY, THAT'S CHEATING! YOU CAN'T BOTH BE STANDING ON THE SAME SURFACE!
I'M NOT STANDEE-ING!
WHAT THE DEVIL?
UH-OH... LOOKS LIKE MY AUNT'S IN ONE OF HER GRUMPY MOODS...
DON'T YOU THINK YOU'RE A BIT BIG TO BE PLAYING LIKE LITTLE GIRLS?
YOU'RE RIGHT, AUNTIE. SORRY.
IS SHE TAKING THE MICKEY?
BRILLIANT!
YAAAY!
YIPPEE!

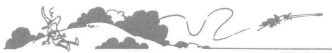

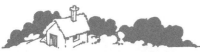

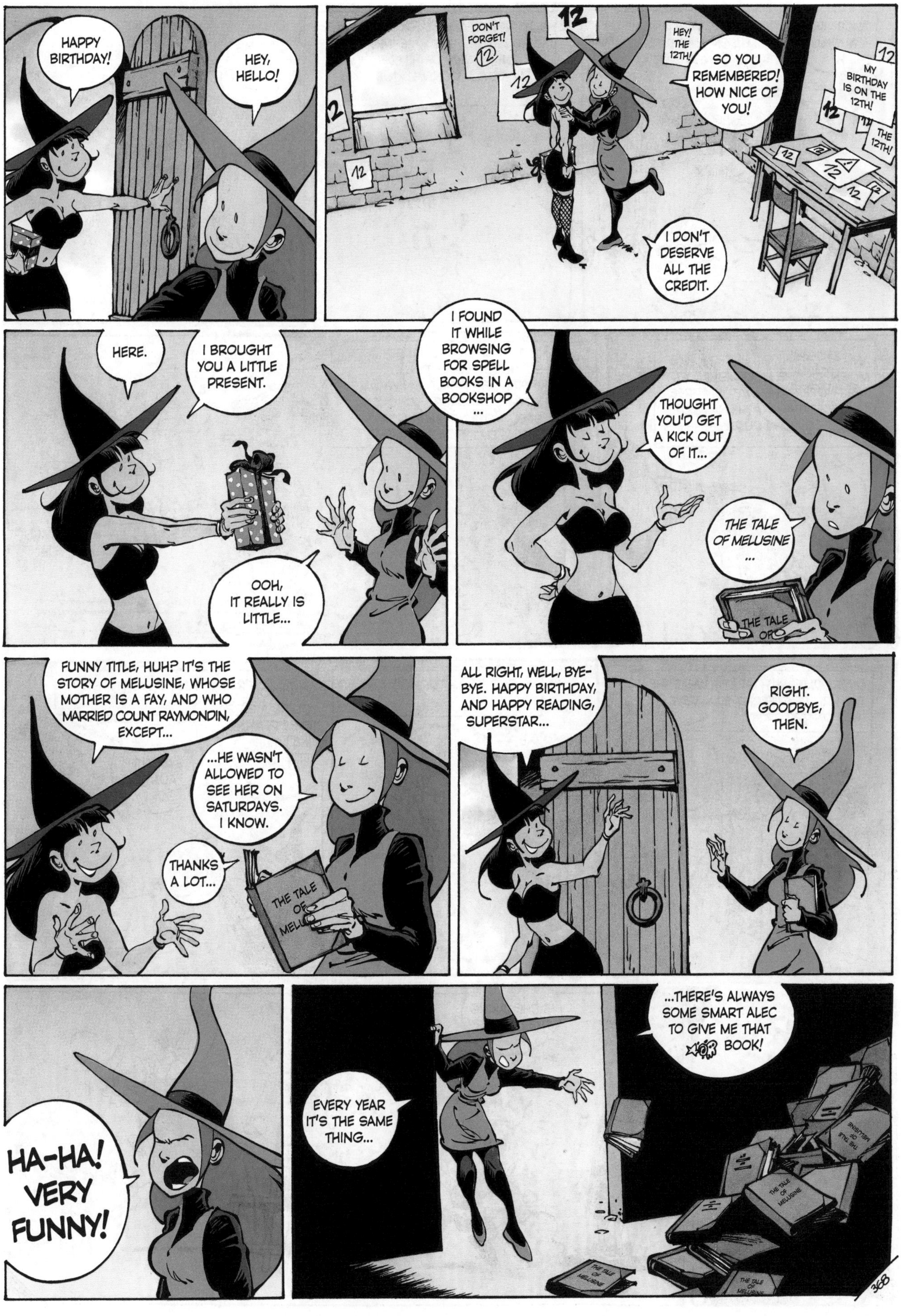
HAPPY BIRTHDAY!
HEY, HELLO!
DON'T FORGET! 12
12
HEY! THE 12TH!
SO YOU REMEMBERED! HOW NICE OF YOU!
MY BIRTHDAY IS ON THE 12TH!
THE 12TH!
I DON'T DESERVE ALL THE CREDIT.
HERE.
I BROUGHT YOU A LITTLE PRESENT.
OOH, IT REALLY IS LITTLE...
I FOUND IT WHILE BROWSING FOR SPELL BOOKS IN A BOOKSHOP ...
THOUGHT YOU'D GET A KICK OUT OF IT...
THE TALE OF MELUSINE ...
FUNNY TITLE, HUH? IT'S THE STORY OF MELUSINE, WHOSE MOTHER IS A FAY, AND WHO MARRIED COUNT RAYMONDIN, EXCEPT...
...HE WASN'T ALLOWED TO SEE HER ON SATURDAYS. I KNOW.
THANKS A LOT...
THE TALE OF MELUSINE
ALL RIGHT, WELL, BYE-BYE. HAPPY BIRTHDAY, AND HAPPY READING, SUPERSTAR...
RIGHT. GOODBYE, THEN.
HA-HA! VERY FUNNY!
EVERY YEAR IT'S THE SAME THING...
...THERE'S ALWAYS SOME SMART ALEC TO GIVE ME THAT BOOK!
THE TALE OF MELUSINE

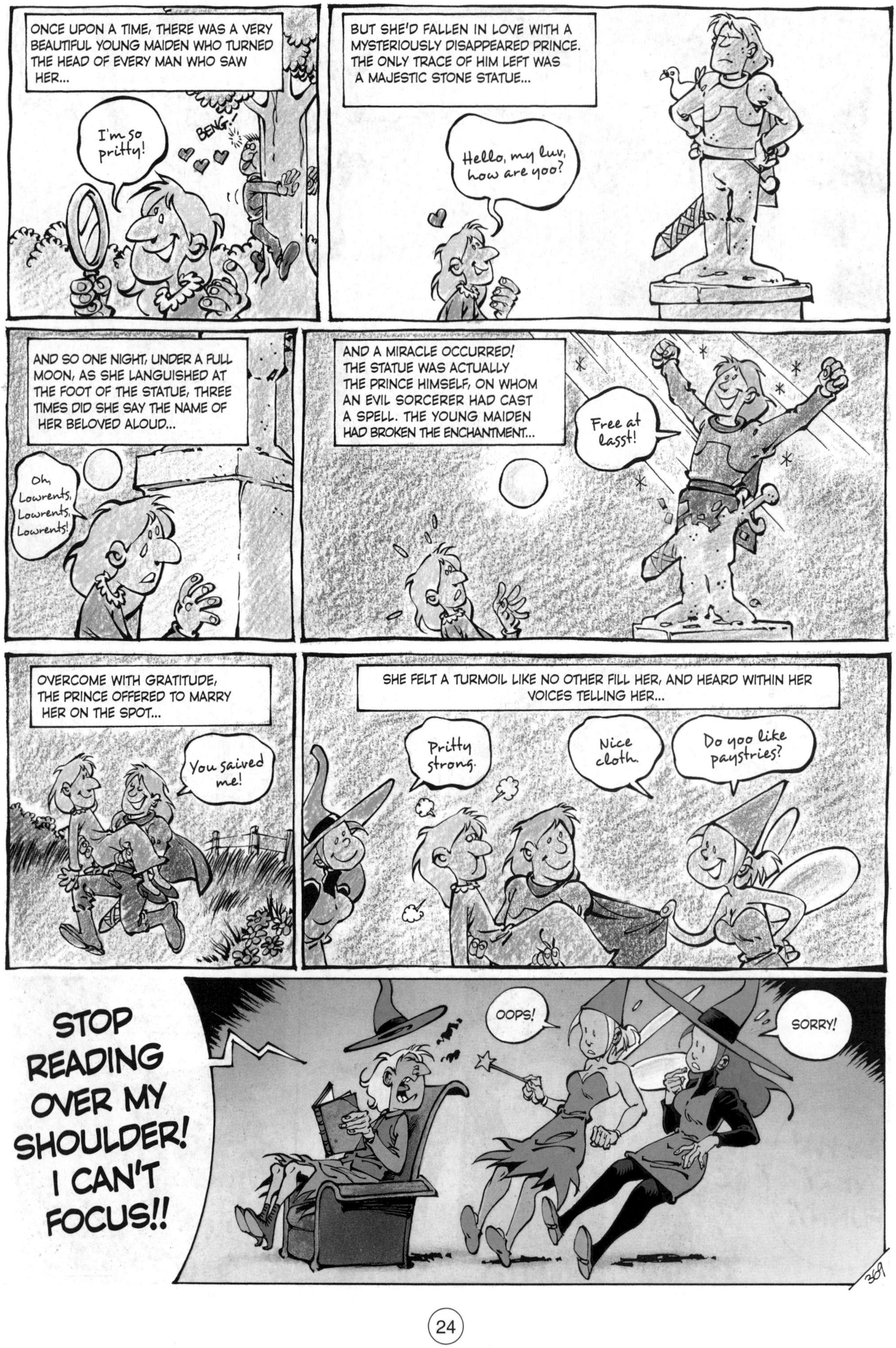
ONCE UPON A TIME, THERE WAS A VERY BEAUTIFUL YOUNG MAIDEN WHO TURNED THE HEAD OF EVERY MAN WHO SAW HER...
I'm so pritty!
BENG!
BUT SHE'D FALLEN IN LOVE WITH A MYSTERIOUSLY DISAPPEARED PRINCE. THE ONLY TRACE OF HIM LEFT WAS A MAJESTIC STONE STATUE...
Hello, my luv, how are yoo?
AND SO ONE NIGHT, UNDER A FULL MOON, AS SHE LANGUISHED AT THE FOOT OF THE STATUE, THREE TIMES DID SHE SAY THE NAME OF HER BELOVED ALOUD...
Oh, Lowrents, Lowrents, Lowrents!
AND A MIRACLE OCCURRED! THE STATUE WAS ACTUALLY THE PRINCE HIMSELF, ON WHOM AN EVIL SORCERER HAD CAST A SPELL. THE YOUNG MAIDEN HAD BROKEN THE ENCHANTMENT...
Free at lasst!
OVERCOME WITH GRATITUDE, THE PRINCE OFFERED TO MARRY HER ON THE SPOT...
You saived me!
SHE FELT A TURMOIL LIKE NO OTHER FILL HER, AND HEARD WITHIN HER VOICES TELLING HER...
Pritty strong.
Nice cloth.
Do yoo like paystries?
STOP READING OVER MY SHOULDER! I CAN'T FOCUS!!
OOPS!
SORRY!

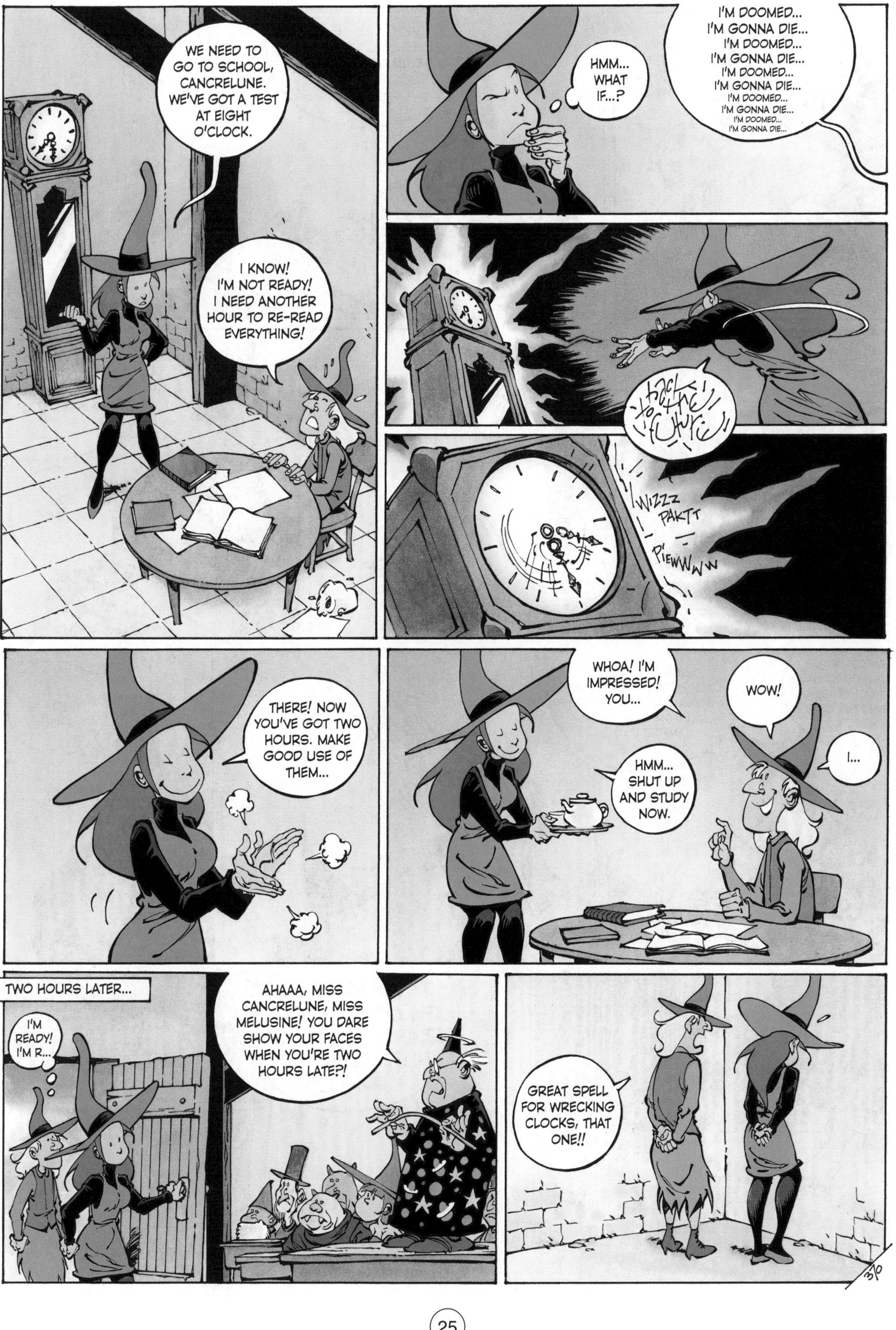
WE NEED TO GO TO SCHOOL, CANCRELUNE. WE'VE GOT A TEST AT EIGHT O'CLOCK.
I KNOW! I'M NOT READY! I NEED ANOTHER HOUR TO RE-READ EVERYTHING!
HMM... WHAT IF...?
I'M DOOMED... I'M GONNA DIE... I'M DOOMED... I'M GONNA DIE... I'M DOOMED... I'M GONNA DIE... I'M DOOMED... I'M GONNA DIE... I'M DOOMED... I'M GONNA DIE...
WIZZZ
PAKTT
PIEWWWW
THERE! NOW YOU'VE GOT TWO HOURS. MAKE GOOD USE OF THEM...
WHOA! I'M IMPRESSED! YOU...
WOW!
HMM... SHUT UP AND STUDY NOW.
I...
TWO HOURS LATER...
I'M READY! I'M R...
AHAAA, MISS CANCRELUNE, MISS MELUSINE! YOU DARE SHOW YOUR FACES WHEN YOU'RE TWO HOURS LATE?!
GREAT SPELL FOR WRECKING CLOCKS, THAT ONE!!

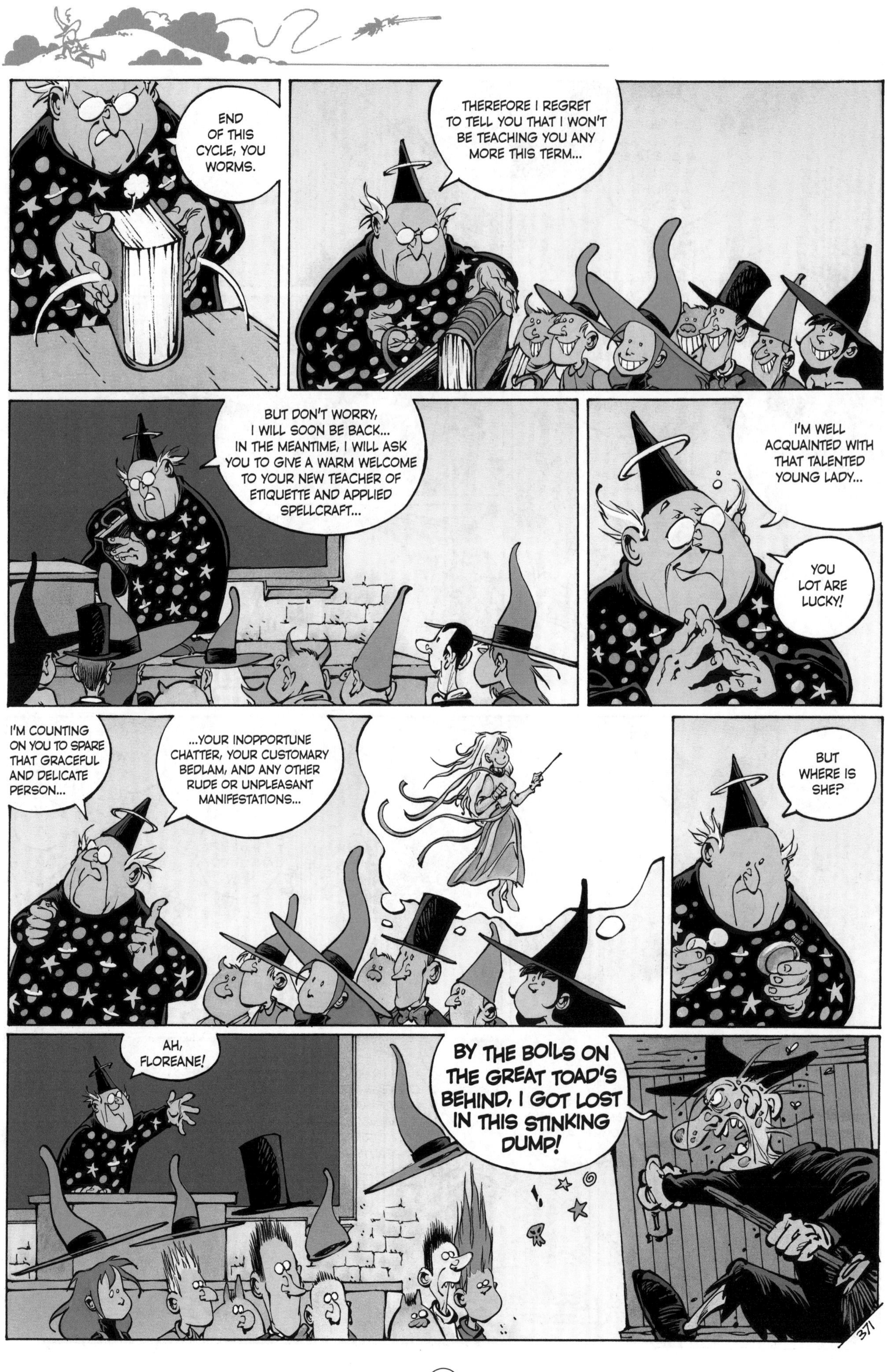
END OF THIS CYCLE, YOU WORMS.
THEREFORE I REGRET TO TELL YOU THAT I WON'T BE TEACHING YOU ANY MORE THIS TERM...
BUT DON'T WORRY, I WILL SOON BE BACK... IN THE MEANTIME, I WILL ASK YOU TO GIVE A WARM WELCOME TO YOUR NEW TEACHER OF ETIQUETTE AND APPLIED SPELLCRAFT...
I'M WELL ACQUAINTED WITH THAT TALENTED YOUNG LADY...
YOU LOT ARE LUCKY!
I'M COUNTING ON YOU TO SPARE THAT GRACEFUL AND DELICATE PERSON...
...YOUR INOPPORTUNE CHATTER, YOUR CUSTOMARY BEDLAM, AND ANY OTHER RUDE OR UNPLEASANT MANIFESTATIONS...
BUT WHERE IS SHE?
AH, FLOREANE!
BY THE BOILS ON THE GREAT TOAD'S BEHIND, I GOT LOST IN THIS STINKING DUMP!

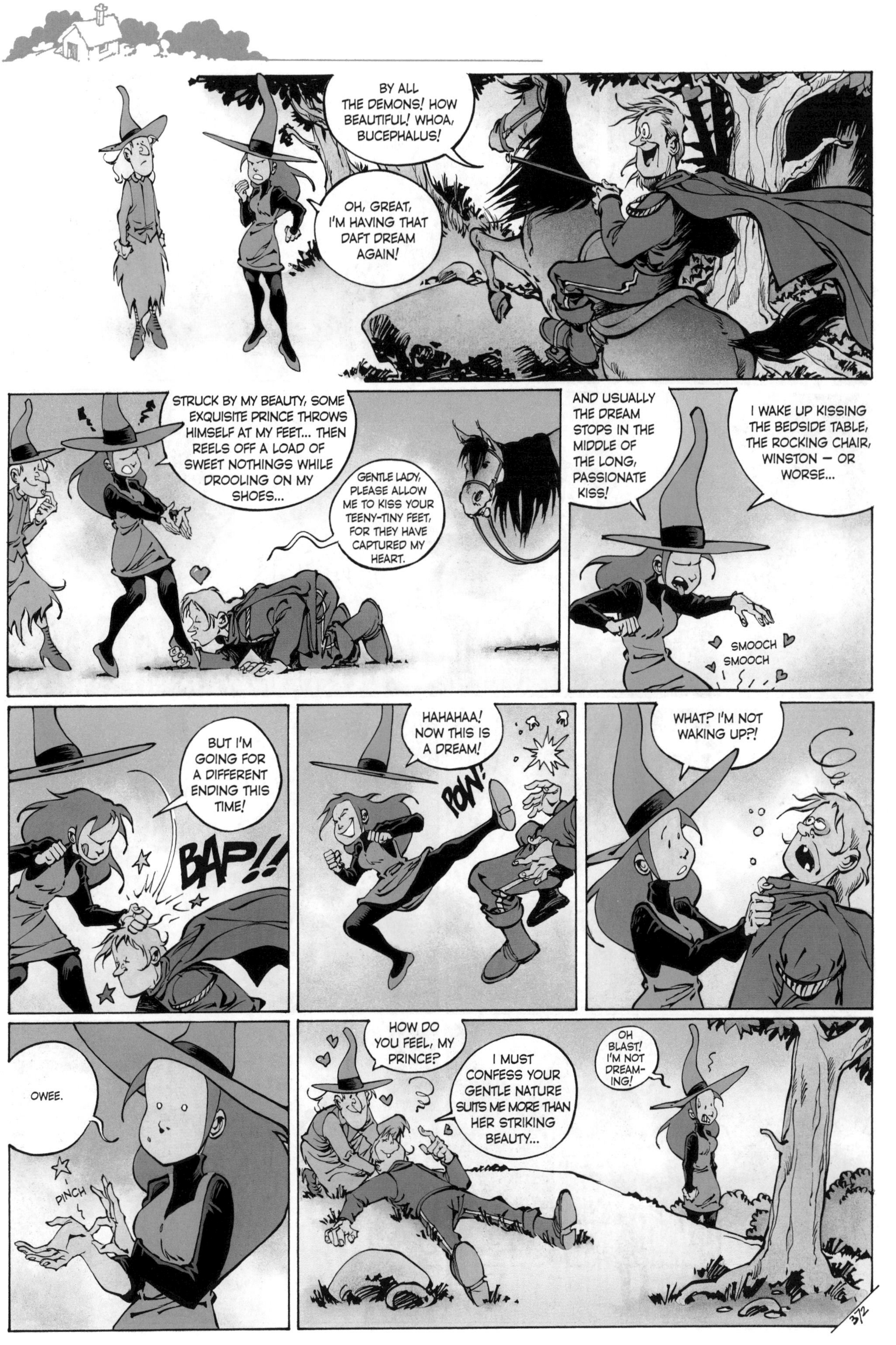

BY ALL THE DEMONS! HOW BEAUTIFUL! WHOA, BUCEPHALUS!
OH, GREAT, I'M HAVING THAT DAFT DREAM AGAIN!
STRUCK BY MY BEAUTY, SOME EXQUISITE PRINCE THROWS HIMSELF AT MY FEET... THEN REELS OFF A LOAD OF SWEET NOTHINGS WHILE DROOLING ON MY SHOES...
GENTLE LADY, PLEASE ALLOW ME TO KISS YOUR TEENY-TINY FEET, FOR THEY HAVE CAPTURED MY HEART.
AND USUALLY THE DREAM STOPS IN THE MIDDLE OF THE LONG, PASSIONATE KISS!
I WAKE UP KISSING THE BEDSIDE TABLE, THE ROCKING CHAIR, WINSTON — OR WORSE...
SMOOCH
SMOOCH
BUT I'M GOING FOR A DIFFERENT ENDING THIS TIME!
BAP!!
HAHAHAA! NOW THIS IS A DREAM!
POW!
WHAT? I'M NOT WAKING UP?!
OWEE.
PINCH
HOW DO YOU FEEL, MY PRINCE?
I MUST CONFESS YOUR GENTLE NATURE SUITS ME MORE THAN HER STRIKING BEAUTY...
OH BLAST! I'M NOT DREAMING!
3/2

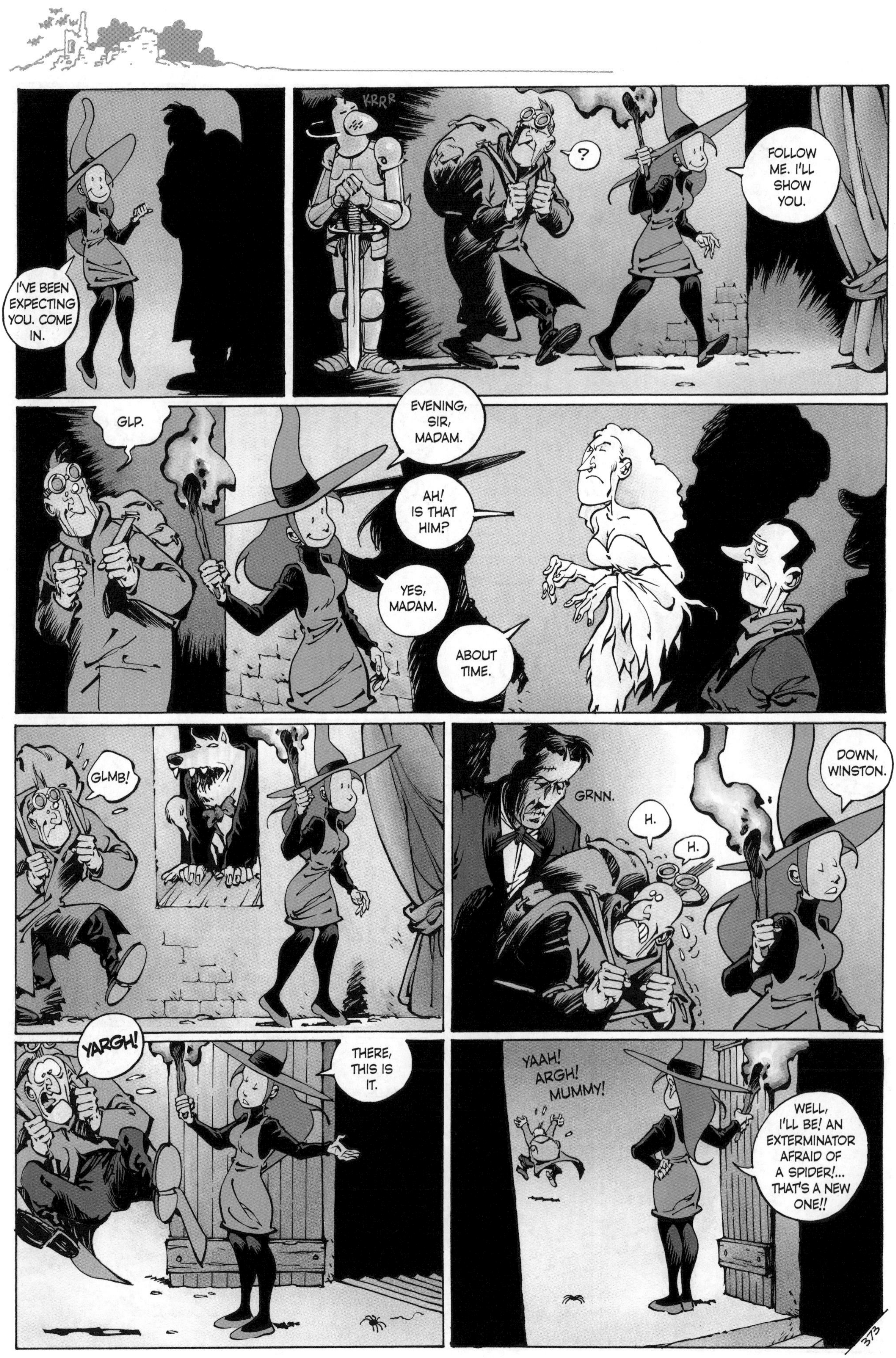
I'VE BEEN EXPECTING YOU. COME IN.
KRRR
?
FOLLOW ME. I'LL SHOW YOU.
GLP.
EVENING, SIR, MADAM.
AH! IS THAT HIM?
YES, MADAM.
ABOUT TIME.
GLMB!
GRNN.
H.
H.
DOWN, WINSTON.
YARGH!
THERE, THIS IS IT.
YAAH! ARGH! MUMMY!
WELL, I'LL BE! AN EXTERMINATOR AFRAID OF A SPIDER!... THAT'S A NEW ONE!!
373

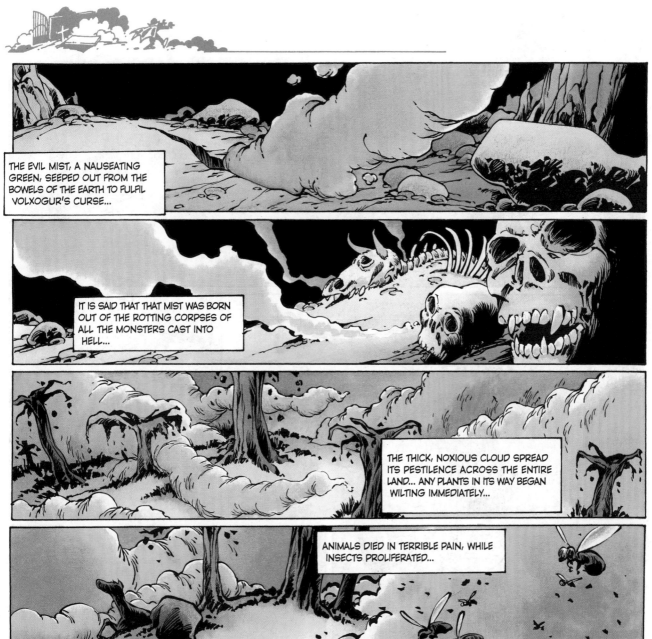

THE EVIL MIST, A NAUSEATING GREEN, SEEPED OUT FROM THE BOWELS OF THE EARTH TO FULFIL VOLXOGUR'S CURSE...

IT IS SAID THAT THAT MIST WAS BORN OUT OF THE ROTTING CORPSES OF ALL THE MONSTERS CAST INTO HELL...

THE THICK, NOXIOUS CLOUD SPREAD ITS PESTILENCE ACROSS THE ENTIRE LAND... ANY PLANTS IN ITS WAY BEGAN WILTING IMMEDIATELY...

ANIMALS DIED IN TERRIBLE PAIN, WHILE INSECTS PROLIFERATED...

THE GREAT SORCERER ARCHANTRAX PIT HIS POWERS AGAINST THE CURSE...

...AND SENT THE ABOMINATION BACK WHENCE IT CAME...

37-A

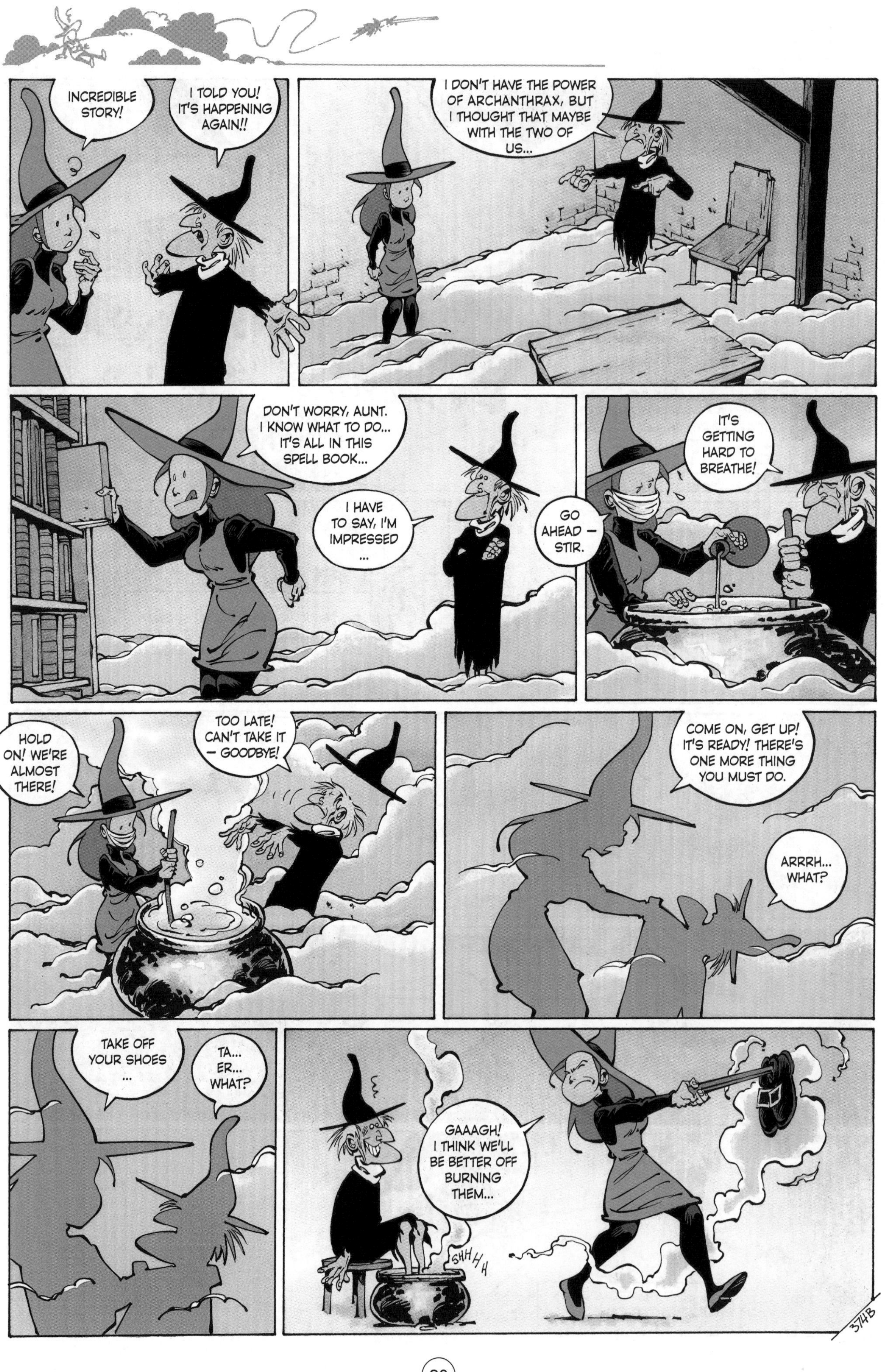

INCREDIBLE STORY!
I TOLD YOU! IT'S HAPPENING AGAIN!!
I DON'T HAVE THE POWER OF ARCHANTHRAX, BUT I THOUGHT THAT MAYBE WITH THE TWO OF US...
DON'T WORRY, AUNT. I KNOW WHAT TO DO... IT'S ALL IN THIS SPELL BOOK...
I HAVE TO SAY, I'M IMPRESSED ...
IT'S GETTING HARD TO BREATHE!
GO AHEAD — STIR.
HOLD ON! WE'RE ALMOST THERE!
TOO LATE! CAN'T TAKE IT — GOODBYE!
COME ON, GET UP! IT'S READY! THERE'S ONE MORE THING YOU MUST DO.
ARRRH... WHAT?
TAKE OFF YOUR SHOES ...
TA... ER... WHAT?
GAAAGH! I THINK WE'LL BE BETTER OFF BURNING THEM...
SHHHH

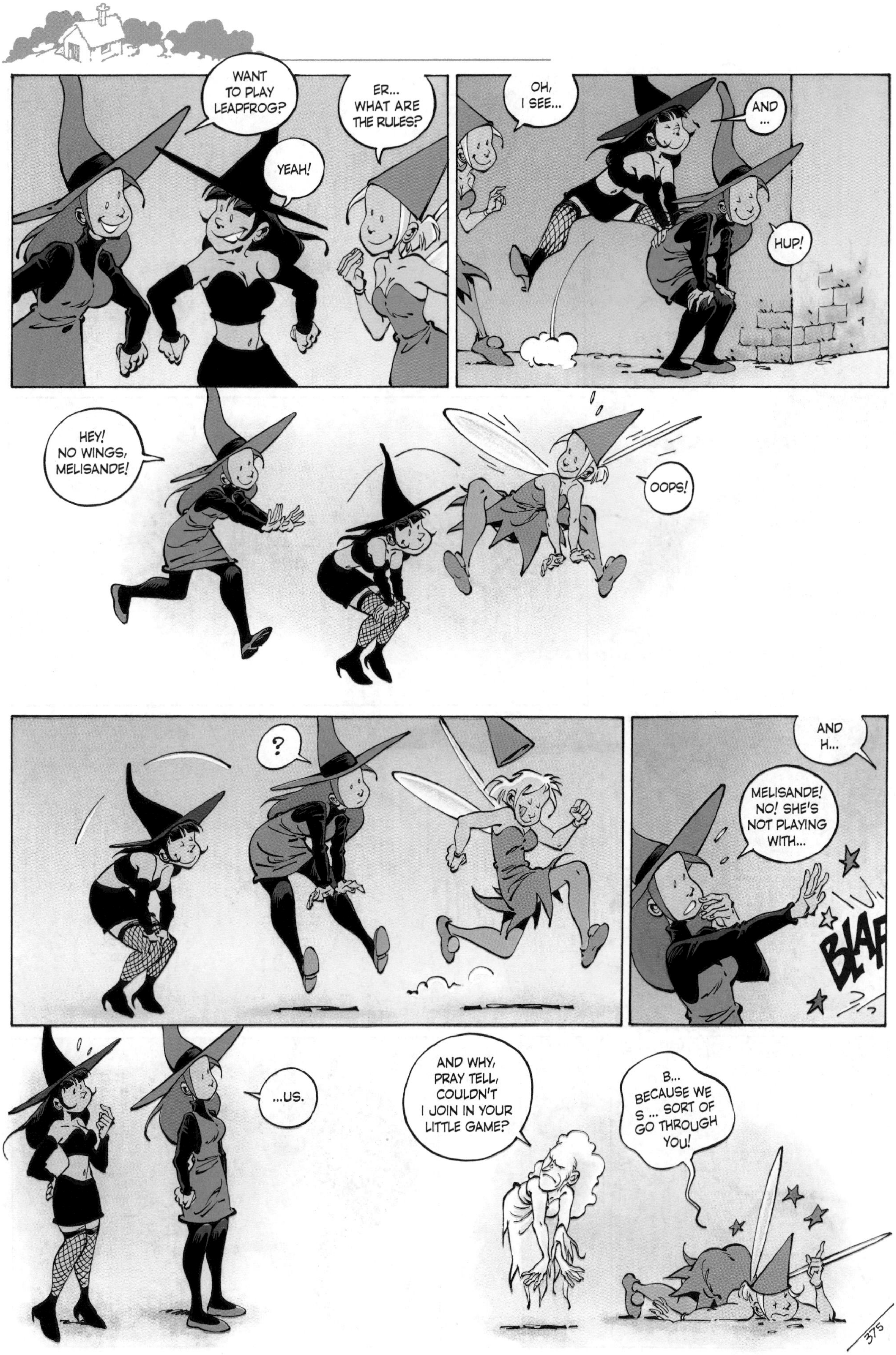
WANT TO PLAY LEAPFROG?
YEAH!
ER... WHAT ARE THE RULES?
OH, I SEE...
AND ...
HUP!
HEY! NO WINGS, MELISANDE!
OOPS!
?
AND H...
MELISANDE! NO! SHE'S NOT PLAYING WITH...
BLAF
...US.
AND WHY, PRAY TELL, COULDN'T I JOIN IN YOUR LITTLE GAME?
B... BECAUSE WE S ... SORT OF GO THROUGH YOU!
375

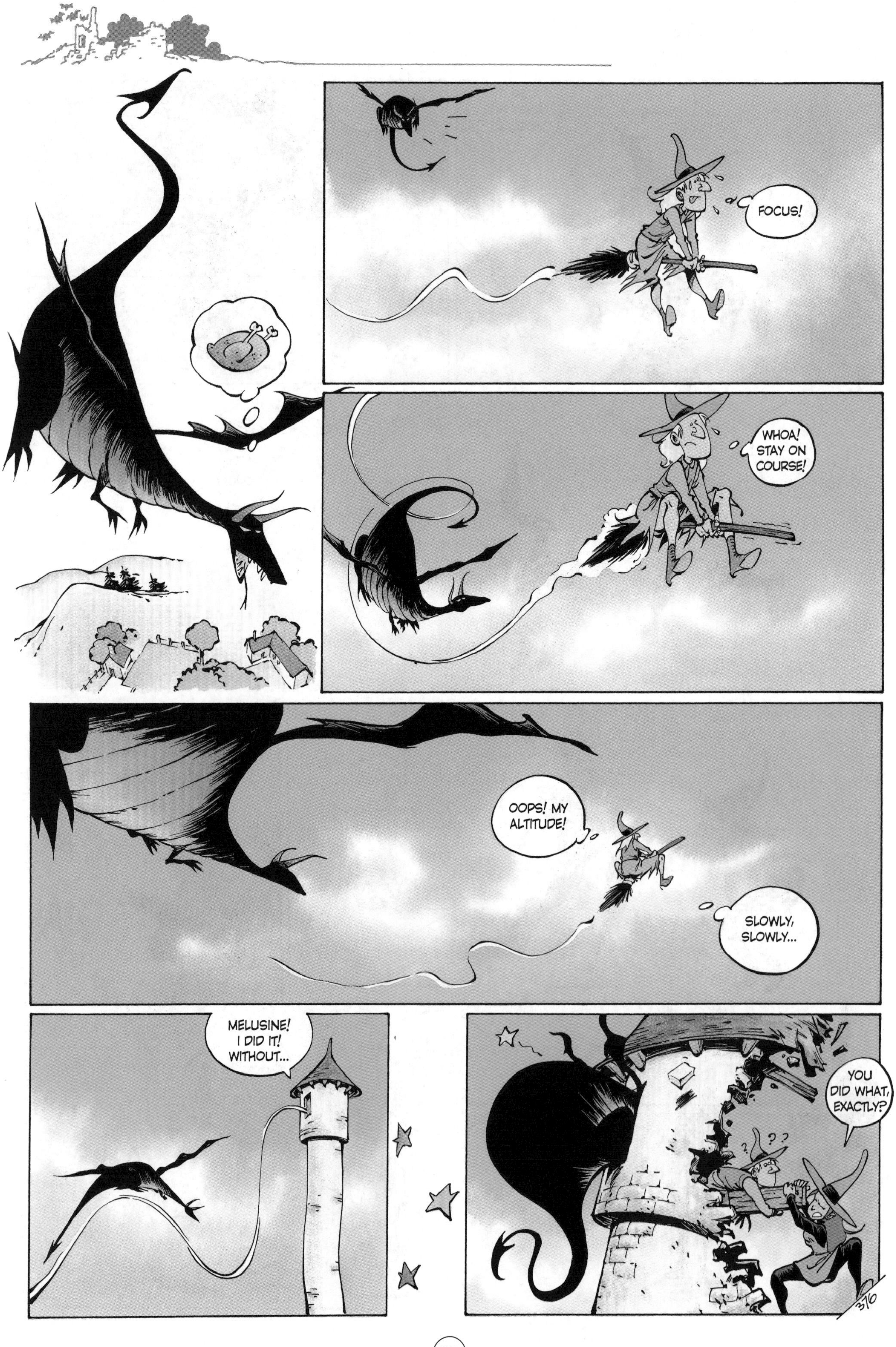
FOCUS!
WHOA! STAY ON COURSE!
OOPS! MY ALTITUDE!
SLOWLY, SLOWLY...
MELUSINE! I DID IT! WITHOUT...
YOU DID WHAT, EXACTLY?

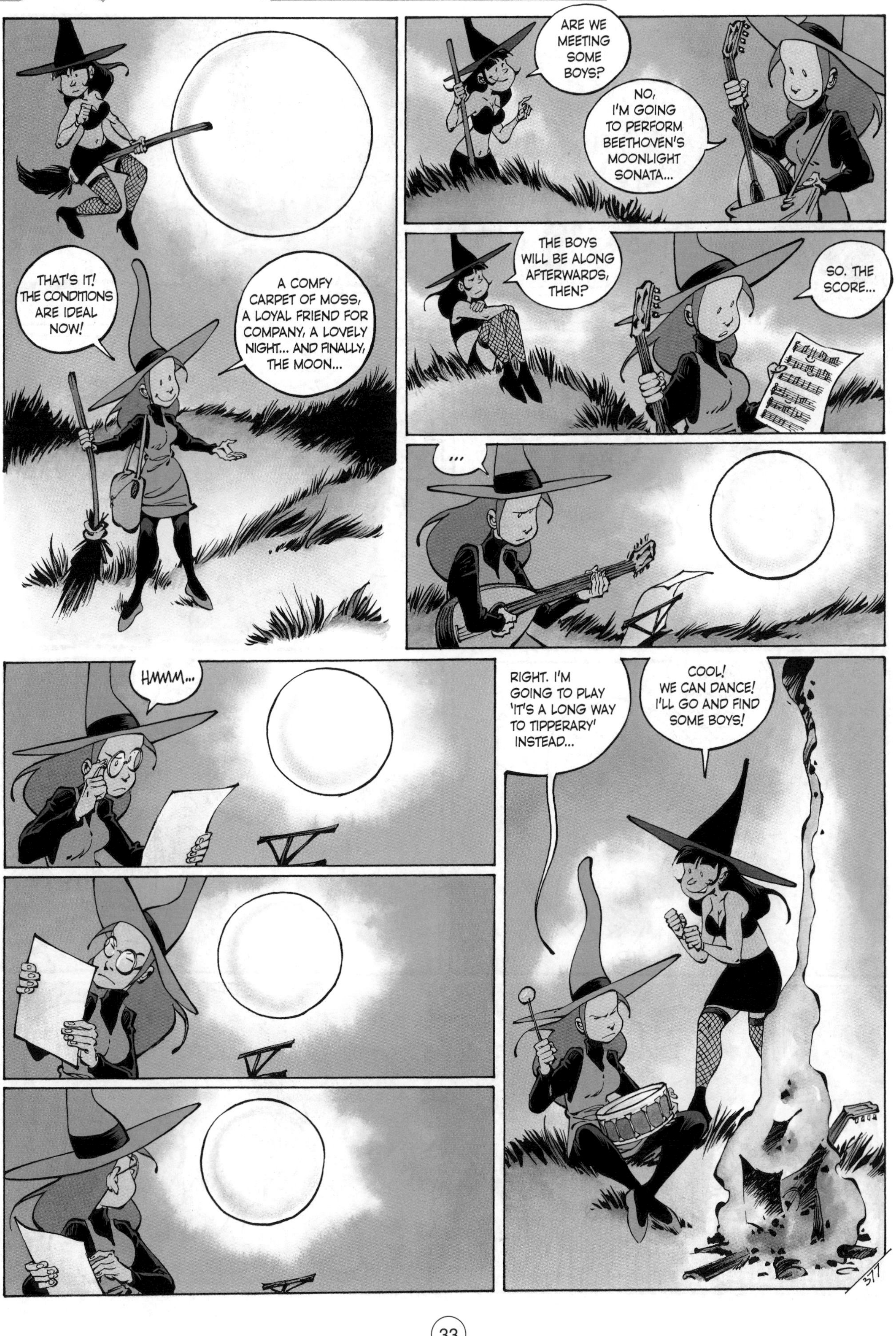
THAT'S IT! THE CONDITIONS ARE IDEAL NOW!
A COMFY CARPET OF MOSS, A LOYAL FRIEND FOR COMPANY, A LOVELY NIGHT... AND FINALLY, THE MOON...
ARE WE MEETING SOME BOYS?
NO, I'M GOING TO PERFORM BEETHOVEN'S MOONLIGHT SONATA...
THE BOYS WILL BE ALONG AFTERWARDS, THEN?
SO. THE SCORE...
...
HMMM...
RIGHT. I'M GOING TO PLAY 'IT'S A LONG WAY TO TIPPERARY' INSTEAD...
COOL! WE CAN DANCE! I'LL GO AND FIND SOME BOYS!

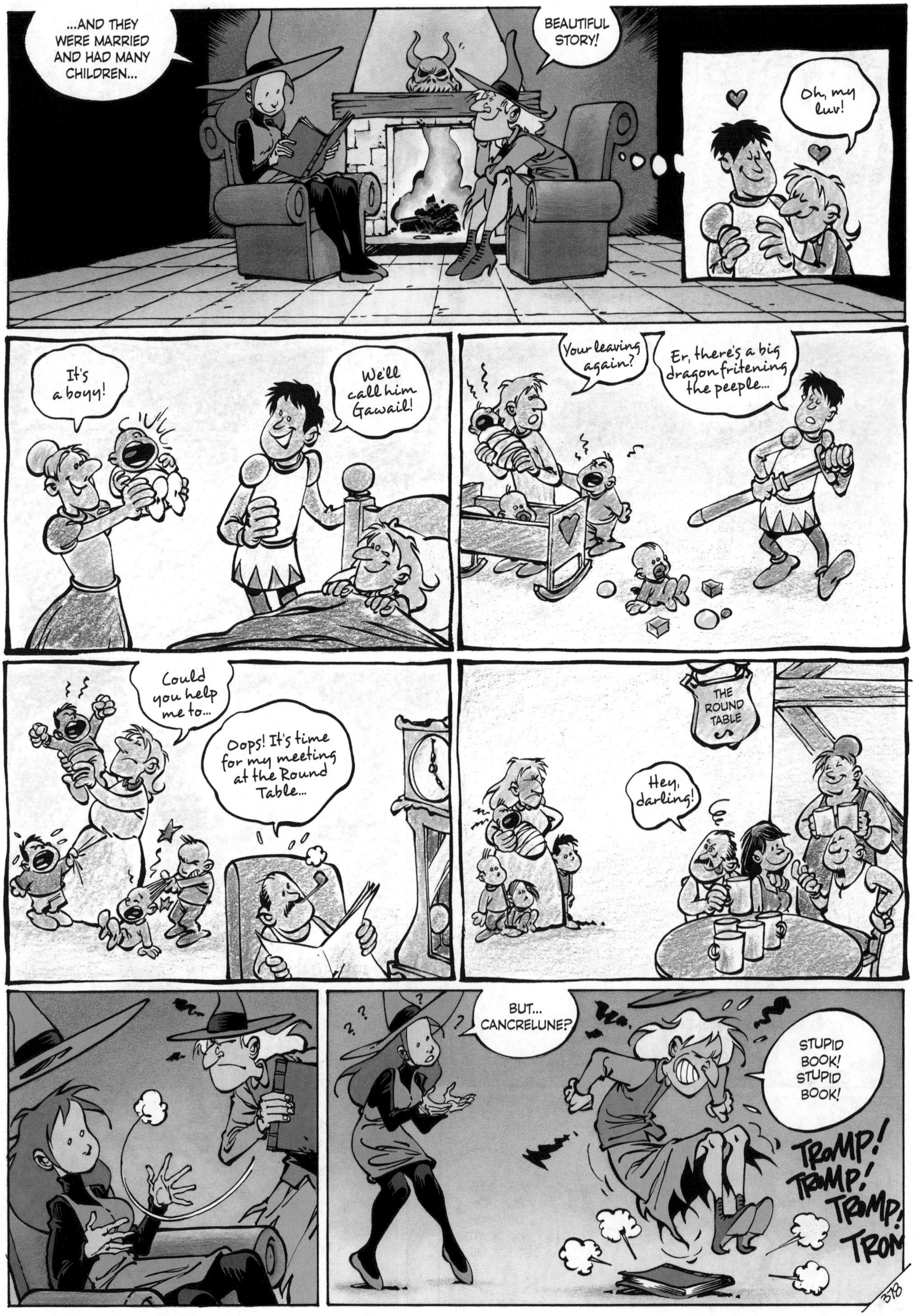
...AND THEY WERE MARRIED AND HAD MANY CHILDREN...
BEAUTIFUL STORY!
Oh, my luv!
It's a boyy!
We'll call him Gawail!
Your leaving again?
Er, there's a big dragon fritening the peeple...
Could you help me to...
Oops! It's time for my meeting at the Round Table...
THE ROUND TABLE
Hey, darling!
BUT... CANCRELUNE?
STUPID BOOK! STUPID BOOK!
TROMP! TROMP! TROMP! TROM

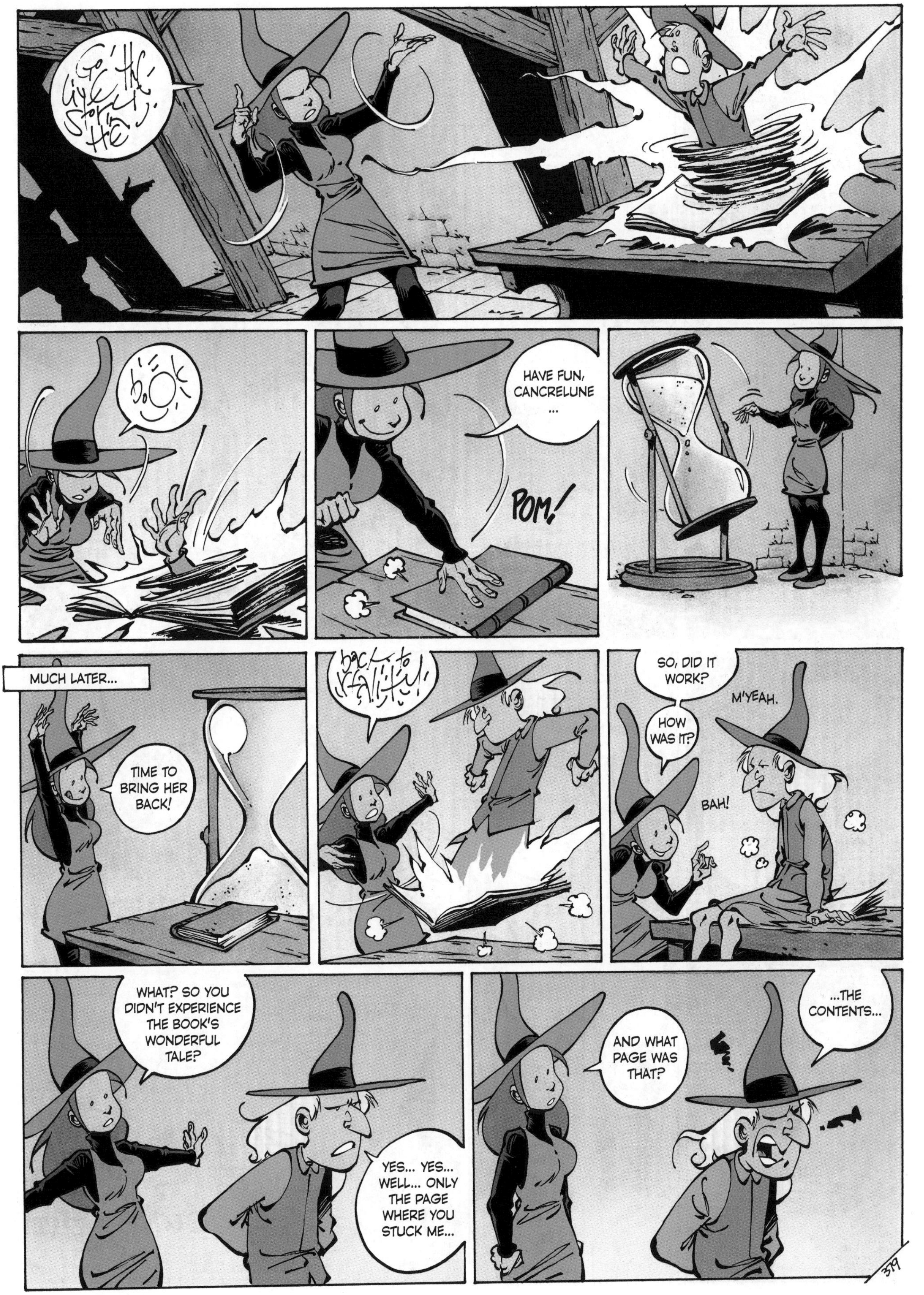

HAVE FUN, CANCRELUNE ...
POM!
MUCH LATER...
TIME TO BRING HER BACK!
SO, DID IT WORK?
HOW WAS IT?
M'YEAH.
BAH!
WHAT? SO YOU DIDN'T EXPERIENCE THE BOOK'S WONDERFUL TALE?
YES... YES... WELL... ONLY THE PAGE WHERE YOU STUCK ME...
AND WHAT PAGE WAS THAT?
...THE CONTENTS...

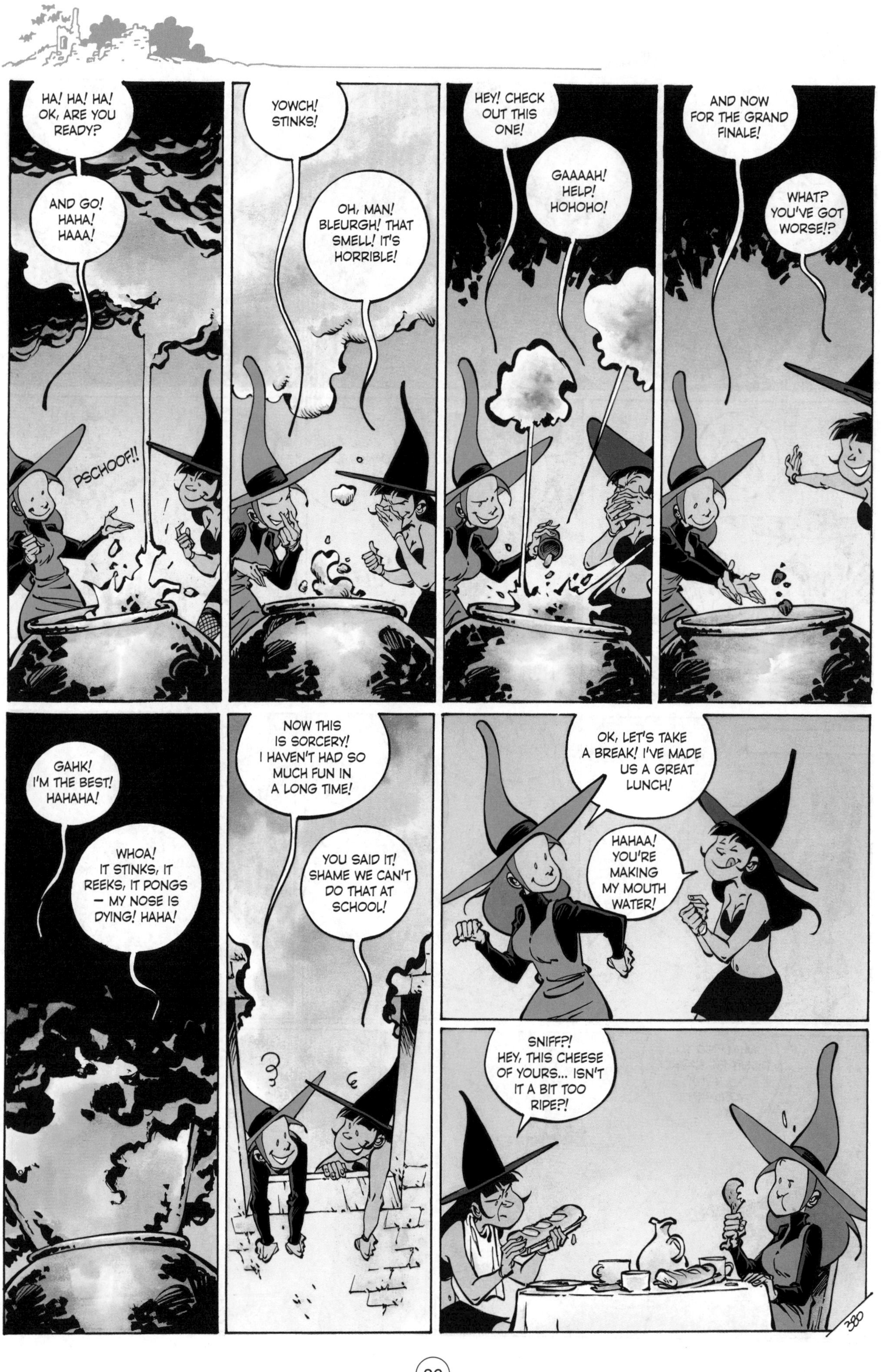
HA! HA! HA! OK, ARE YOU READY?
AND GO! HAHA! HAAA!
PSCHOOF!!
YOWCH! STINKS!
OH, MAN! BLEURGH! THAT SMELL! IT'S HORRIBLE!
HEY! CHECK OUT THIS ONE!
GAAAAH! HELP! HOHOHO!
AND NOW FOR THE GRAND FINALE!
WHAT? YOU'VE GOT WORSE!?
GAHK! I'M THE BEST! HAHAHA!
WHOA! IT STINKS, IT REEKS, IT PONGS – MY NOSE IS DYING! HAHA!
NOW THIS IS SORCERY! I HAVEN'T HAD SO MUCH FUN IN A LONG TIME!
YOU SAID IT! SHAME WE CAN'T DO THAT AT SCHOOL!
OK, LET'S TAKE A BREAK! I'VE MADE US A GREAT LUNCH!
HAHAA! YOU'RE MAKING MY MOUTH WATER!
SNIFF?! HEY, THIS CHEESE OF YOURS... ISN'T IT A BIT TOO RIPE?!

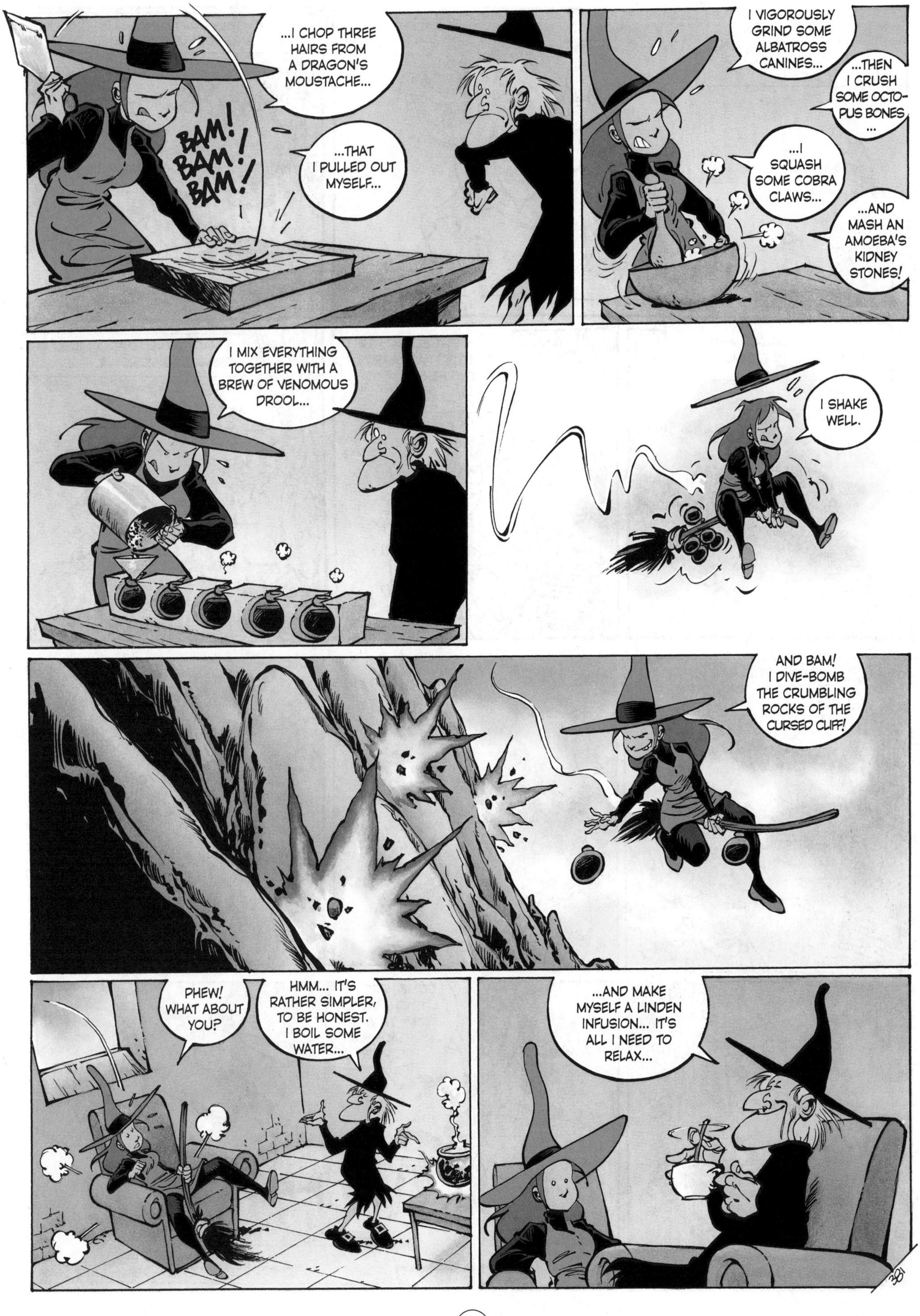
...I CHOP THREE HAIRS FROM A DRAGON'S MOUSTACHE...
BAM! BAM! BAM!
...THAT I PULLED OUT MYSELF...
I VIGOROUSLY GRIND SOME ALBATROSS CANINES...
...THEN I CRUSH SOME OCTO-PUS BONES...
...I SQUASH SOME COBRA CLAWS...
...AND MASH AN AMOEBA'S KIDNEY STONES!
I MIX EVERYTHING TOGETHER WITH A BREW OF VENOMOUS DROOL...
I SHAKE WELL.
AND BAM! I DIVE-BOMB THE CRUMBLING ROCKS OF THE CURSED CLIFF!
PHEW! WHAT ABOUT YOU?
HMM... IT'S RATHER SIMPLER, TO BE HONEST. I BOIL SOME WATER...
...AND MAKE MYSELF A LINDEN INFUSION... IT'S ALL I NEED TO RELAX...

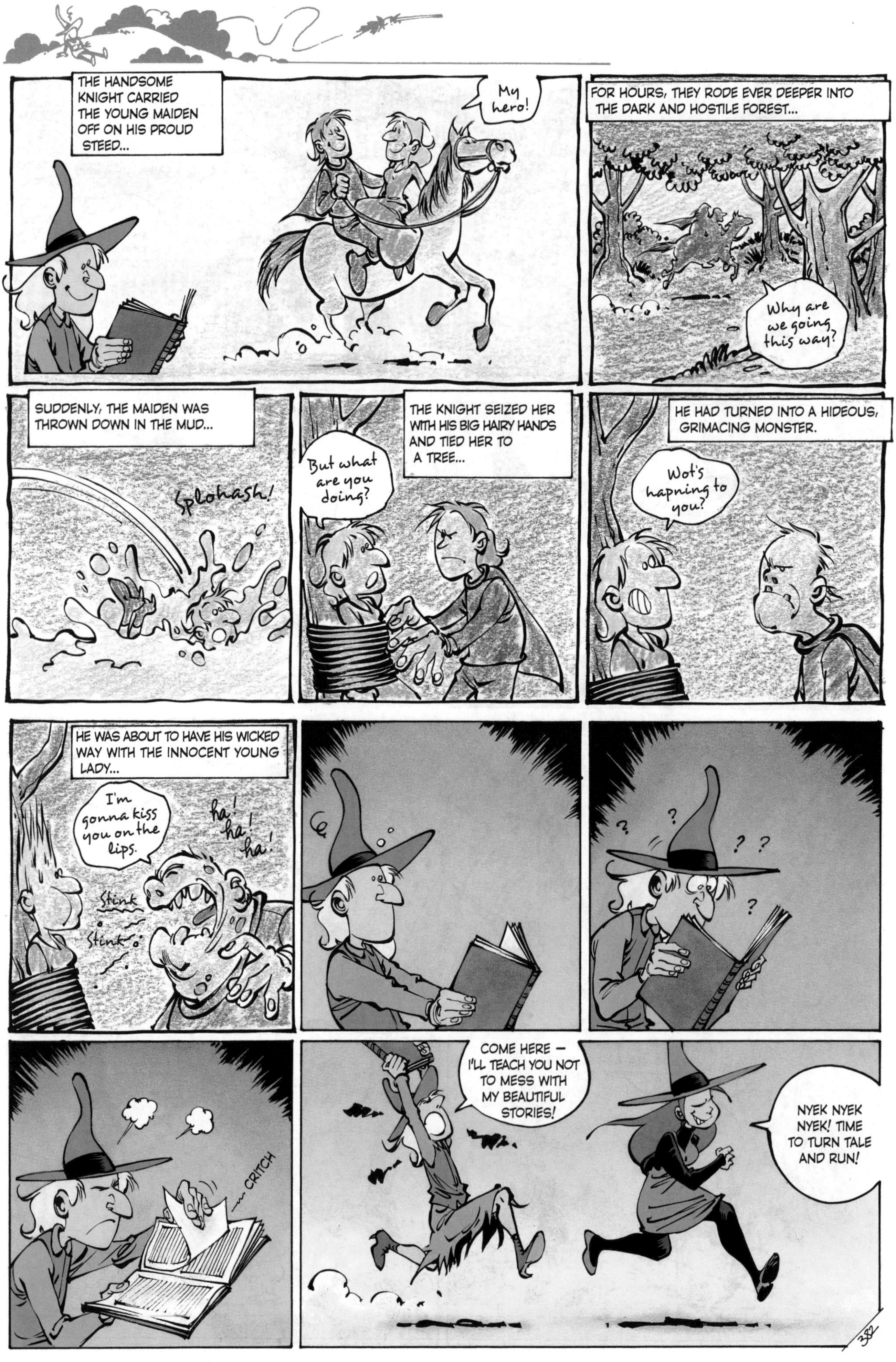
THE HANDSOME KNIGHT CARRIED THE YOUNG MAIDEN OFF ON HIS PROUD STEED...
My hero!
FOR HOURS, THEY RODE EVER DEEPER INTO THE DARK AND HOSTILE FOREST...
Why are we going this way?
SUDDENLY, THE MAIDEN WAS THROWN DOWN IN THE MUD...
Splohash!
THE KNIGHT SEIZED HER WITH HIS BIG HAIRY HANDS AND TIED HER TO A TREE...
But what are you doing?
HE HAD TURNED INTO A HIDEOUS, GRIMACING MONSTER.
Wot's hapning to you?
HE WAS ABOUT TO HAVE HIS WICKED WAY WITH THE INNOCENT YOUNG LADY...
I'm gonna kiss you on the lips.
ha! ha! ha!
Stink
Stink
CRITCH
COME HERE – I'LL TEACH YOU NOT TO MESS WITH MY BEAUTIFUL STORIES!
NYEK NYEK NYEK! TIME TO TURN TALE AND RUN!

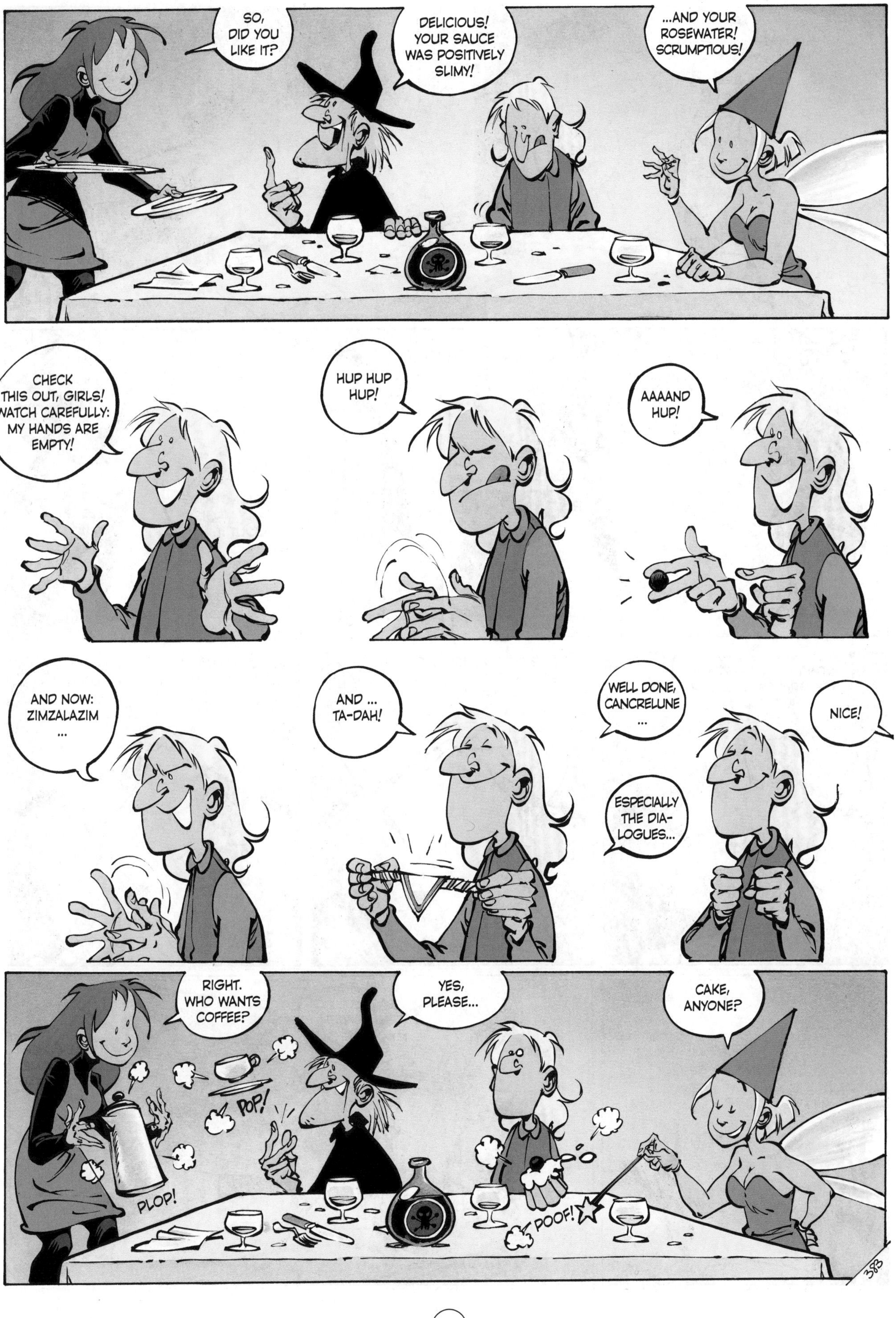
SO, DID YOU LIKE IT?
DELICIOUS! YOUR SAUCE WAS POSITIVELY SLIMY!
...AND YOUR ROSEWATER! SCRUMPTIOUS!
CHECK THIS OUT, GIRLS! WATCH CAREFULLY: MY HANDS ARE EMPTY!
HUP HUP HUP!
AAAAND HUP!
AND NOW: ZIMZALAZIM ...
AND ... TA-DAH!
WELL DONE, CANCRELUNE ...
NICE!
ESPECIALLY THE DIA-LOGUES...
RIGHT. WHO WANTS COFFEE?
YES, PLEASE...
CAKE, ANYONE?
POP!
PLOP!
POOF!

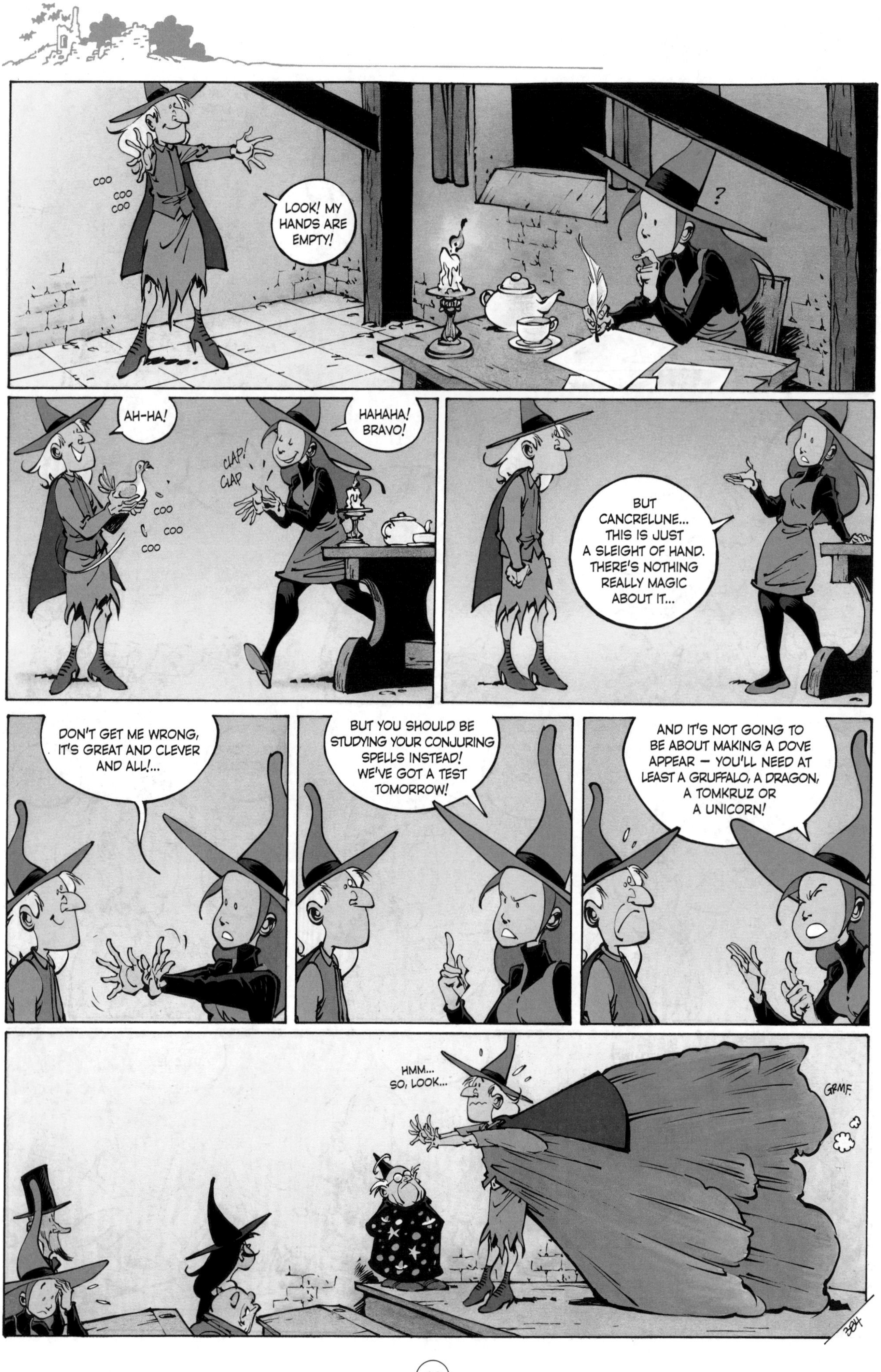
COO
COO
COO
LOOK! MY HANDS ARE EMPTY!
?
AH-HA!
COO
COO
COO
HAHAHA! BRAVO!
CLAP! CLAP
BUT CANCRELUNE... THIS IS JUST A SLEIGHT OF HAND. THERE'S NOTHING REALLY MAGIC ABOUT IT...
DON'T GET ME WRONG, IT'S GREAT AND CLEVER AND ALL!...
BUT YOU SHOULD BE STUDYING YOUR CONJURING SPELLS INSTEAD! WE'VE GOT A TEST TOMORROW!
AND IT'S NOT GOING TO BE ABOUT MAKING A DOVE APPEAR — YOU'LL NEED AT LEAST A GRUFFALO, A DRAGON, A TOMKRUZ OR A UNICORN!
HMM... SO, LOOK...
GRMF.

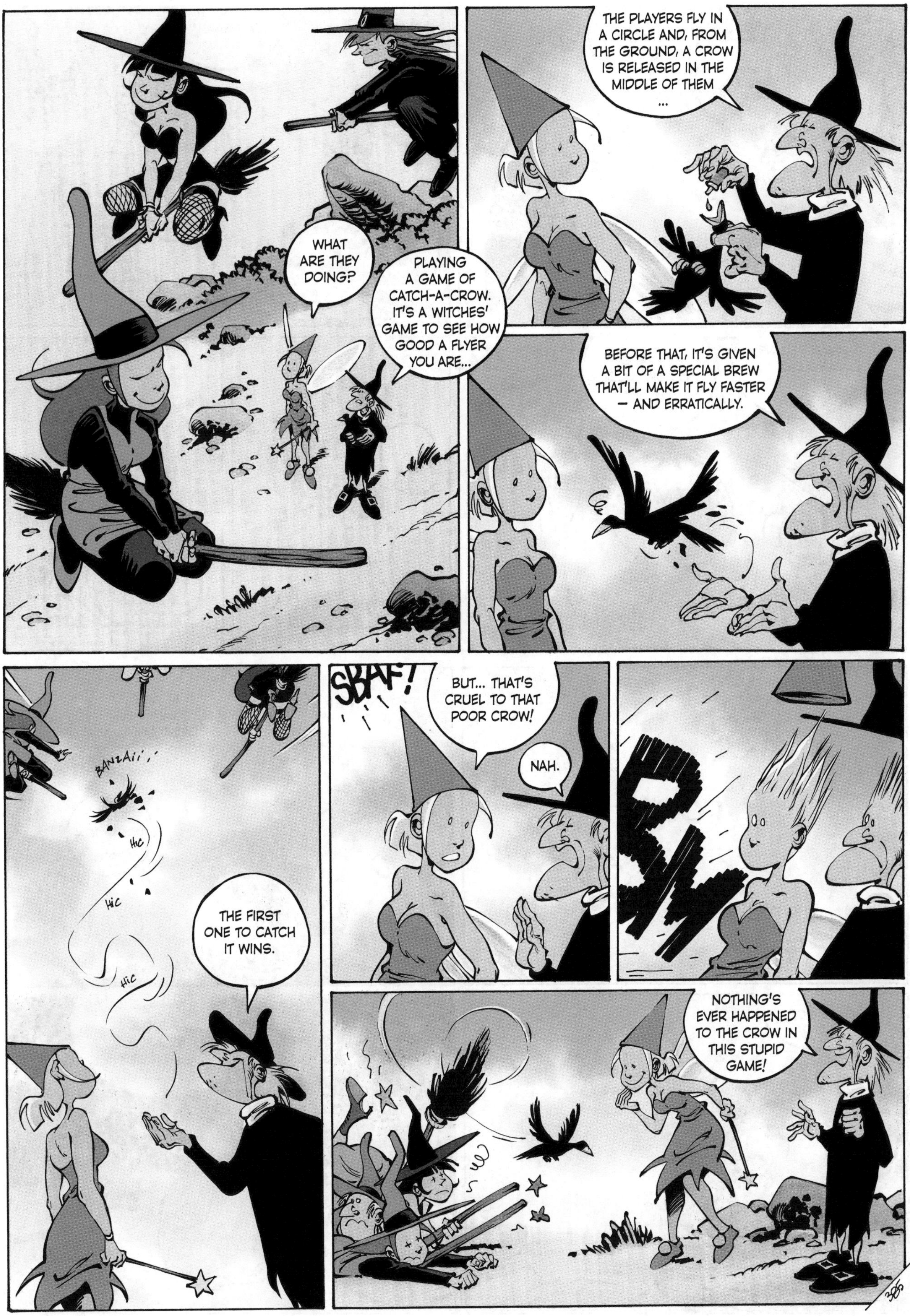
WHAT ARE THEY DOING?
PLAYING A GAME OF CATCH-A-CROW. IT'S A WITCHES' GAME TO SEE HOW GOOD A FLYER YOU ARE...
THE PLAYERS FLY IN A CIRCLE AND, FROM THE GROUND, A CROW IS RELEASED IN THE MIDDLE OF THEM ...
BEFORE THAT, IT'S GIVEN A BIT OF A SPECIAL BREW THAT'LL MAKE IT FLY FASTER — AND ERRATICALLY.
BANZAII
HIC
HIC
HIC
THE FIRST ONE TO CATCH IT WINS.
SBAF!
BUT... THAT'S CRUEL TO THAT POOR CROW!
NAH.
BAM
NOTHING'S EVER HAPPENED TO THE CROW IN THIS STUPID GAME!

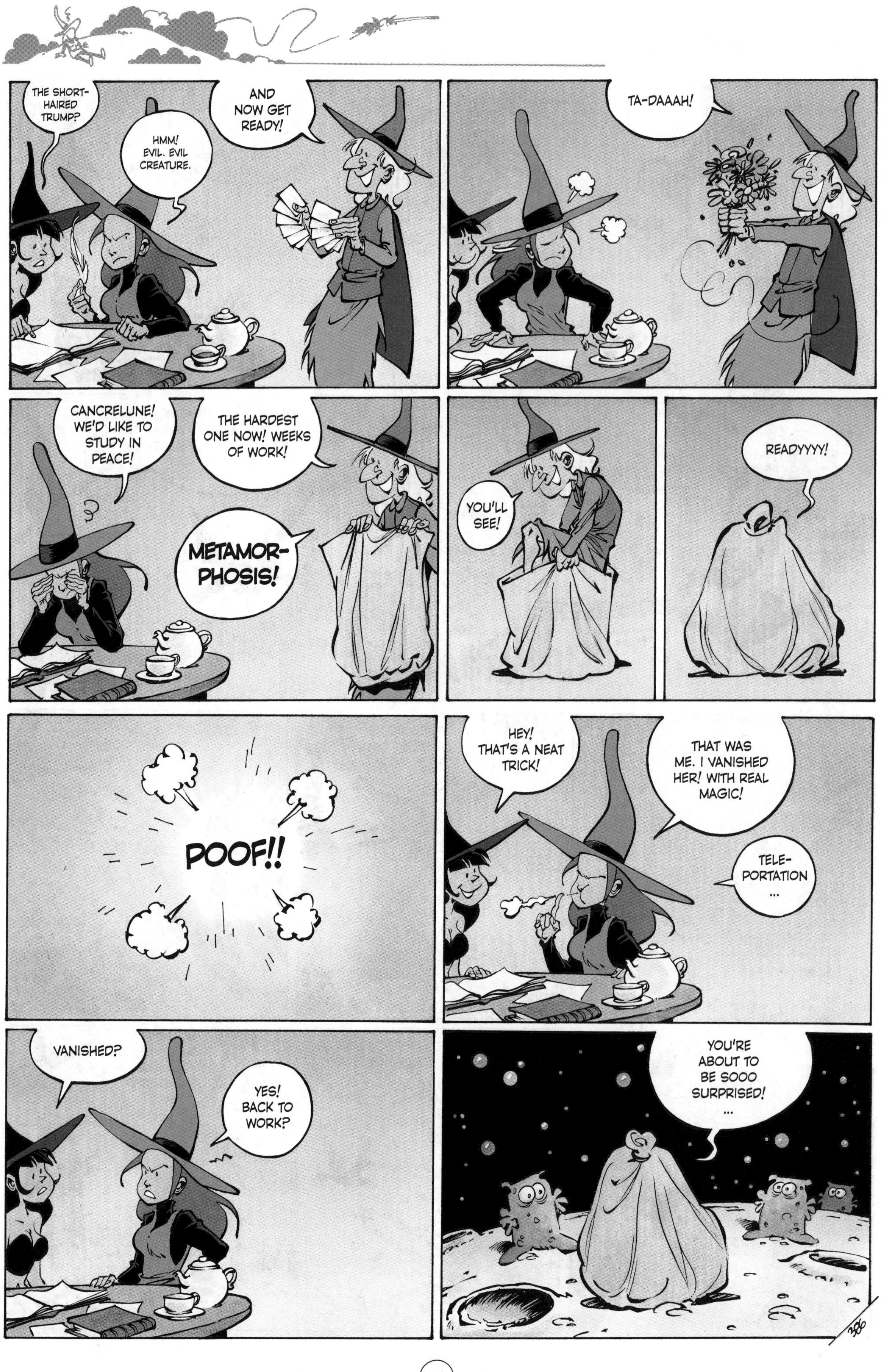
THE SHORT-HAIRED TRUMP?
HMM! EVIL. EVIL CREATURE.
AND NOW GET READY!
TA-DAAAH!
CANCRELUNE! WE'D LIKE TO STUDY IN PEACE!
THE HARDEST ONE NOW! WEEKS OF WORK!
METAMOR-PHOSIS!
YOU'LL SEE!
READYYYY!
POOF!!
HEY! THAT'S A NEAT TRICK!
THAT WAS ME. I VANISHED HER! WITH REAL MAGIC!
TELE-PORTATION ...
VANISHED?
YES! BACK TO WORK?
YOU'RE ABOUT TO BE SOOO SURPRISED! ...

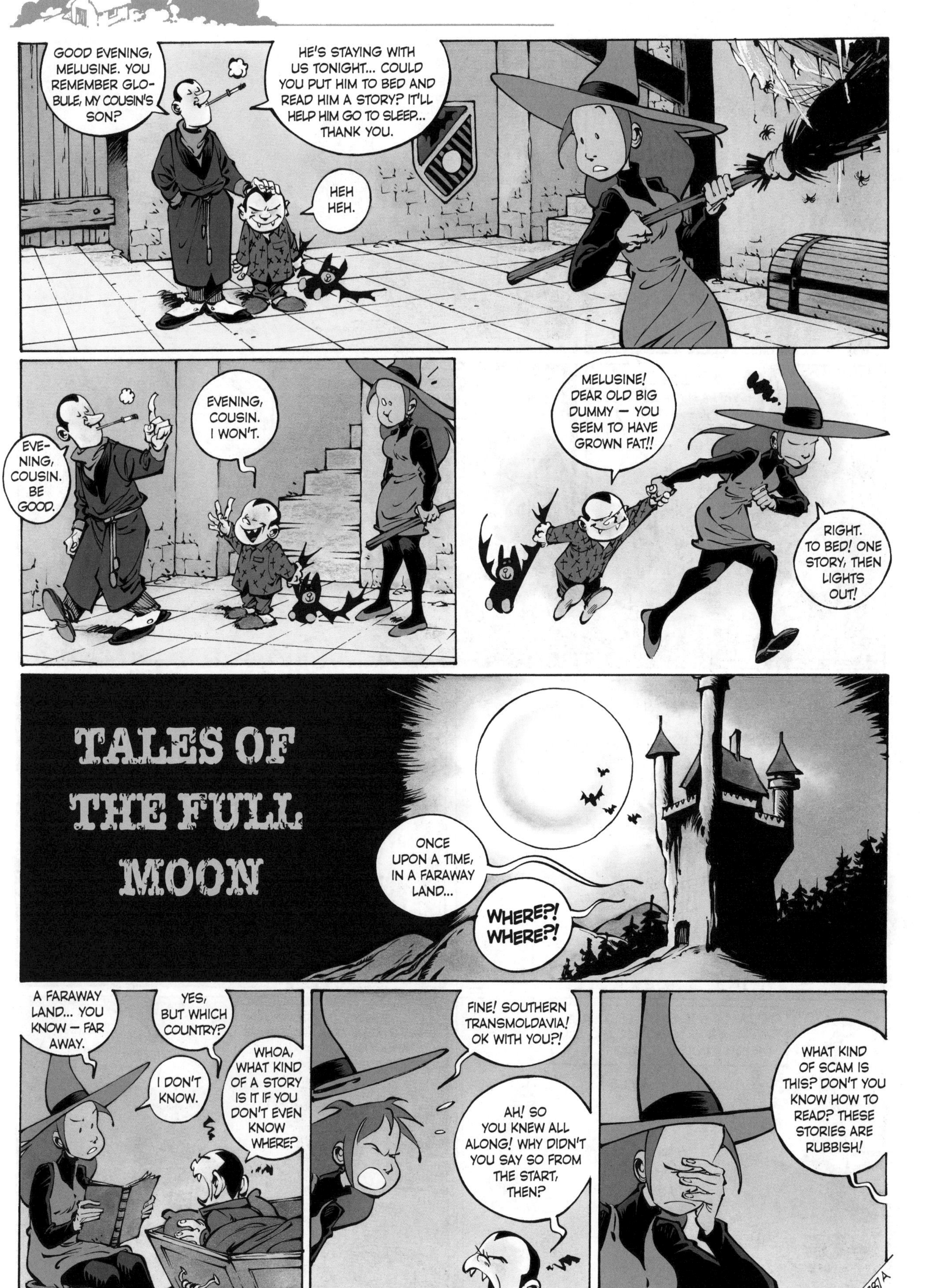

GOOD EVENING, MELUSINE. YOU REMEMBER GLO-BULE, MY COUSIN'S SON?
HE'S STAYING WITH US TONIGHT... COULD YOU PUT HIM TO BED AND READ HIM A STORY? IT'LL HELP HIM GO TO SLEEP... THANK YOU.
HEH HEH.
EVE-NING, COUSIN. BE GOOD.
EVENING, COUSIN. I WON'T.
MELUSINE! DEAR OLD BIG DUMMY — YOU SEEM TO HAVE GROWN FAT!!
RIGHT. TO BED! ONE STORY, THEN LIGHTS OUT!
TALES OF THE FULL MOON
ONCE UPON A TIME, IN A FARAWAY LAND...
WHERE?! WHERE?!
A FARAWAY LAND... YOU KNOW — FAR AWAY.
YES, BUT WHICH COUNTRY?
I DON'T KNOW.
WHOA, WHAT KIND OF A STORY IS IT IF YOU DON'T EVEN KNOW WHERE?
FINE! SOUTHERN TRANSMOLDAVIA! OK WITH YOU?!
AH! SO YOU KNEW ALL ALONG! WHY DIDN'T YOU SAY SO FROM THE START, THEN?
WHAT KIND OF SCAM IS THIS? DON'T YOU KNOW HOW TO READ? THESE STORIES ARE RUBBISH!

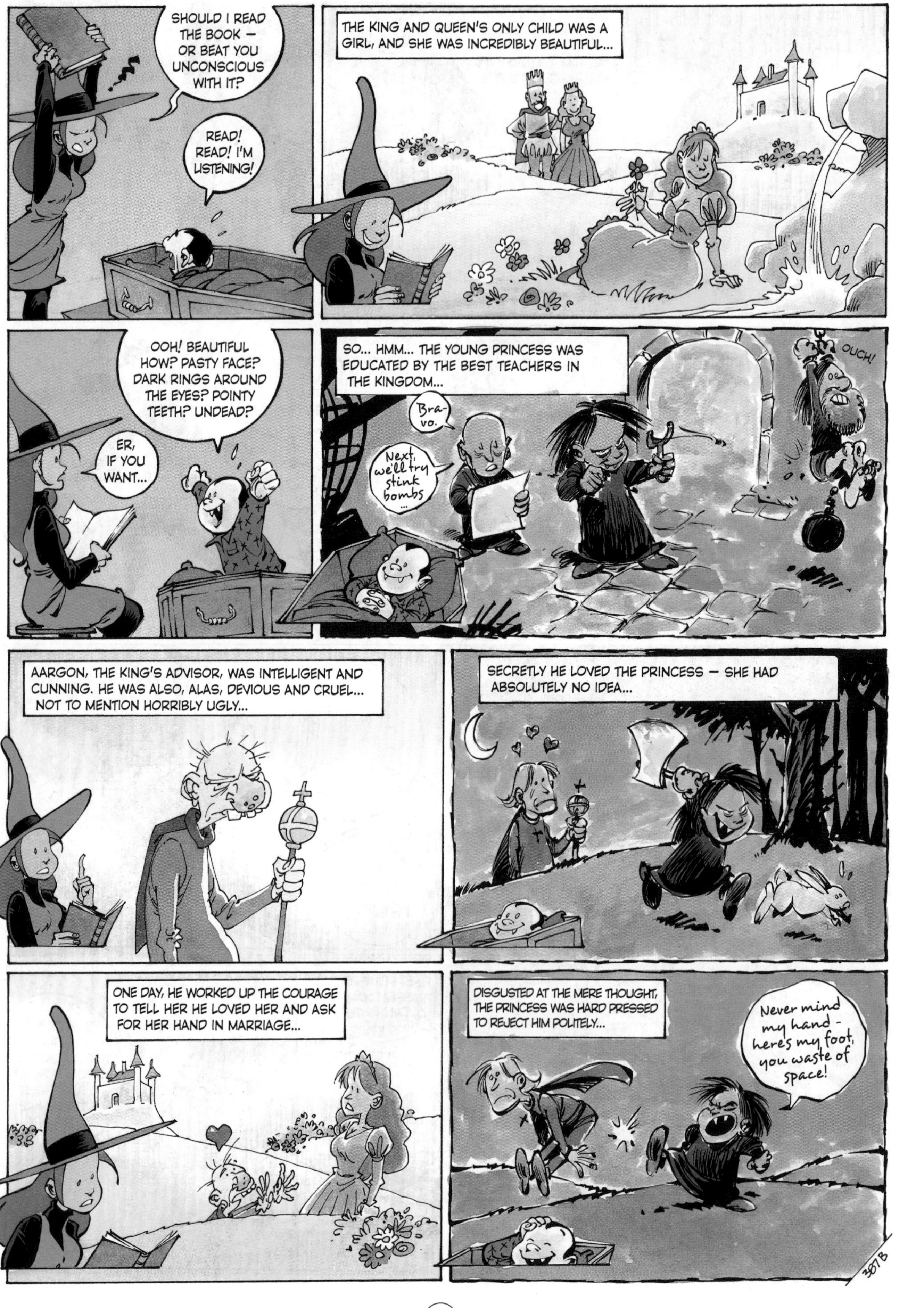
SHOULD I READ THE BOOK — OR BEAT YOU UNCONSCIOUS WITH IT?
READ! READ! I'M LISTENING!
THE KING AND QUEEN'S ONLY CHILD WAS A GIRL, AND SHE WAS INCREDIBLY BEAUTIFUL...
OOH! BEAUTIFUL HOW? PASTY FACE? DARK RINGS AROUND THE EYES? POINTY TEETH? UNDEAD?
ER, IF YOU WANT...
SO... HMM... THE YOUNG PRINCESS WAS EDUCATED BY THE BEST TEACHERS IN THE KINGDOM...
Bra-vo.
Next, we'll try stink bombs...
OUCH!
AARGON, THE KING'S ADVISOR, WAS INTELLIGENT AND CUNNING. HE WAS ALSO, ALAS, DEVIOUS AND CRUEL... NOT TO MENTION HORRIBLY UGLY...
SECRETLY HE LOVED THE PRINCESS — SHE HAD ABSOLUTELY NO IDEA...
ONE DAY, HE WORKED UP THE COURAGE TO TELL HER HE LOVED HER AND ASK FOR HER HAND IN MARRIAGE...
DISGUSTED AT THE MERE THOUGHT, THE PRINCESS WAS HARD PRESSED TO REJECT HIM POLITELY...
Never mind my hand - here's my foot, you waste of space!

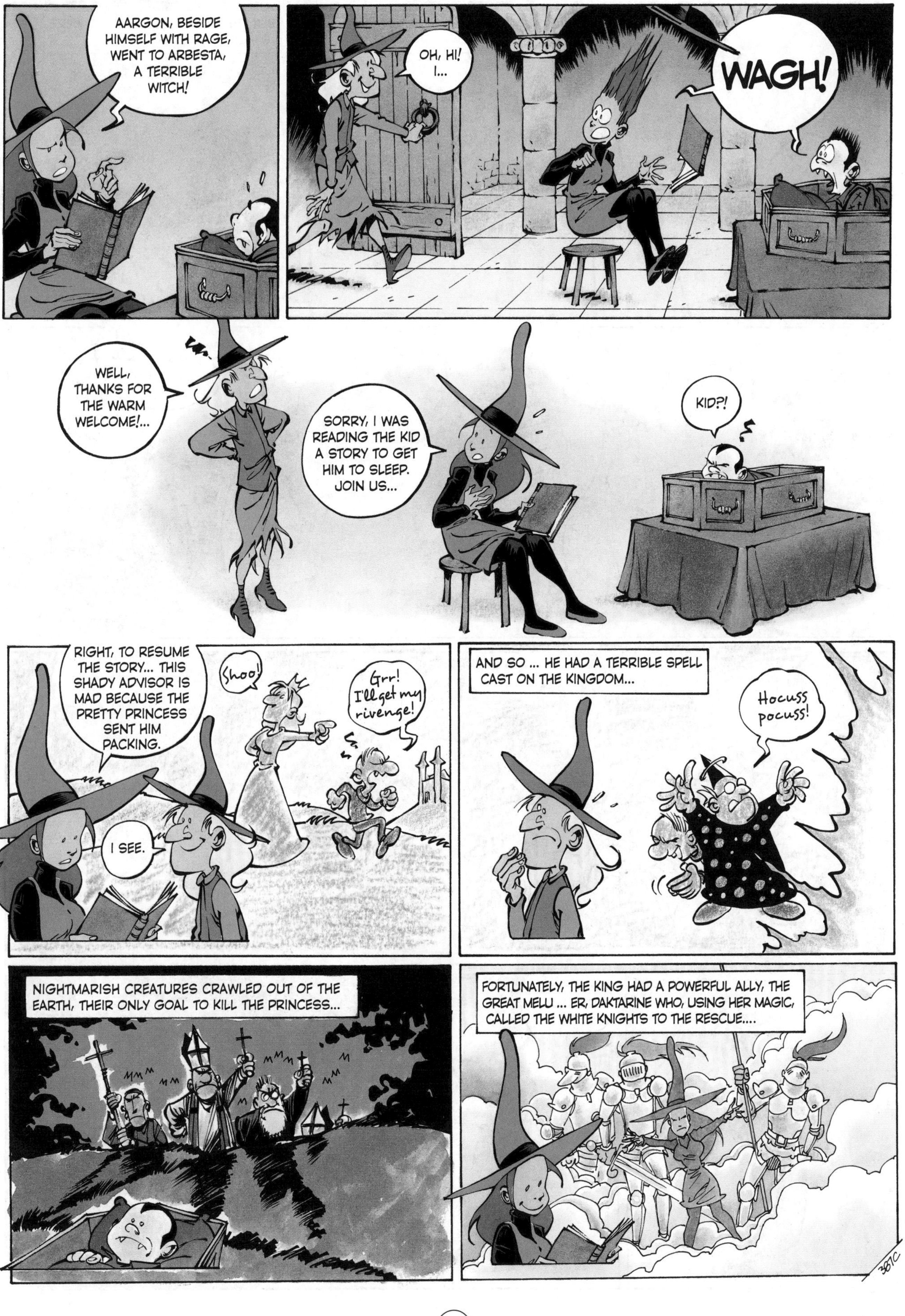
AARGON, BESIDE HIMSELF WITH RAGE, WENT TO ARBESTA, A TERRIBLE WITCH!
OH, HI! I...
WAGH!
WELL, THANKS FOR THE WARM WELCOME!...
SORRY, I WAS READING THE KID A STORY TO GET HIM TO SLEEP. JOIN US...
KID?!
RIGHT, TO RESUME THE STORY... THIS SHADY ADVISOR IS MAD BECAUSE THE PRETTY PRINCESS SENT HIM PACKING.
Shoo!
Grr! I'll get my rivenge!
I SEE.
AND SO ... HE HAD A TERRIBLE SPELL CAST ON THE KINGDOM...
Hocuss pocuss!
NIGHTMARISH CREATURES CRAWLED OUT OF THE EARTH, THEIR ONLY GOAL TO KILL THE PRINCESS...
FORTUNATELY, THE KING HAD A POWERFUL ALLY, THE GREAT MELU ... ER, DAKTARINE WHO, USING HER MAGIC, CALLED THE WHITE KNIGHTS TO THE RESCUE....

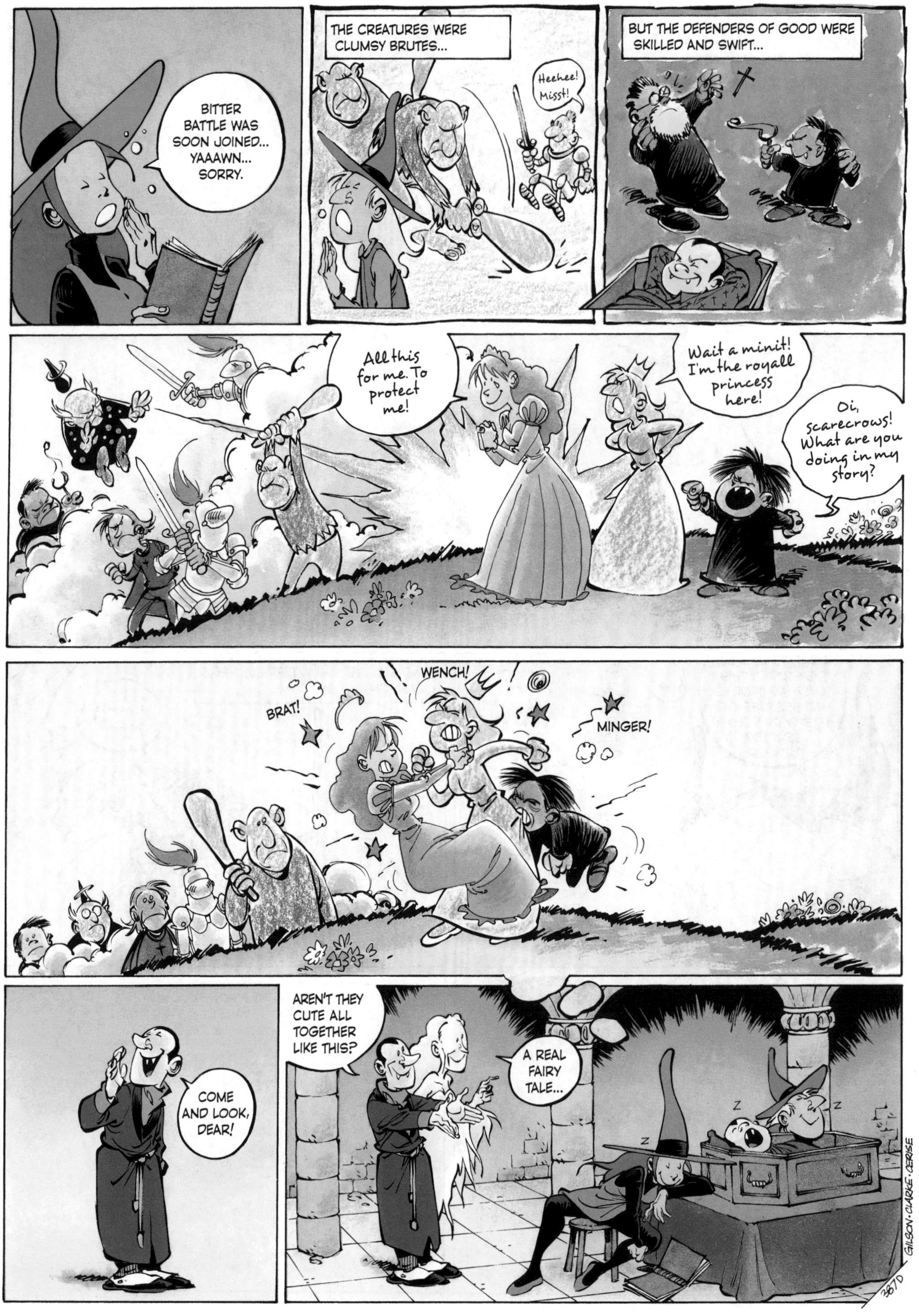
BITTER BATTLE WAS SOON JOINED... YAAAWN... SORRY.
THE CREATURES WERE CLUMSY BRUTES...
Heehee! Misst!
BUT THE DEFENDERS OF GOOD WERE SKILLED AND SWIFT...
All this for me. To protect me!
Wait a minit! I'm the royall princess here!
Oi, scarecrows! What are you doing in my story?
WENCH!
BRAT!
MINGER!
COME AND LOOK, DEAR!
AREN'T THEY CUTE ALL TOGETHER LIKE THIS?
A REAL FAIRY TALE...
Z
Z
Z
GILSON · CLARKE · CERISE

Coming soon

clarke · gilson
Melusine
6
In Witching School
CINEBOOK
The 9th Art Publisher

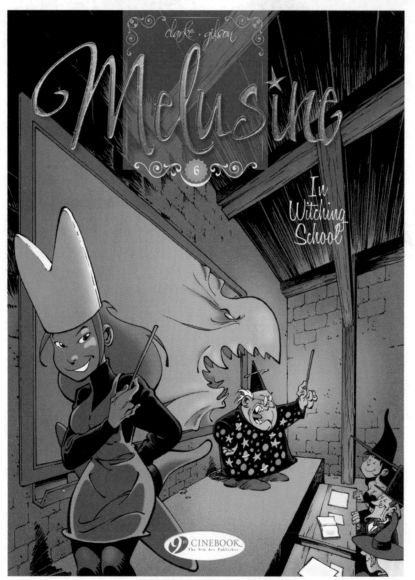

6 - In Witching School

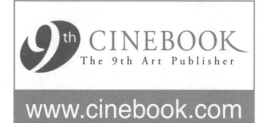